The Conquering of Tate the Pious

FAR HOPE STORIES

SIERRA SIMONE

The Conquering of Tate the Pious

SIERRA SIMONE

One

TATE

1068

THERE WAS no grass greener than graveyard grass.

No matter the season, the weather, the biting wind or the burning sun, the grass in the large abbey graveyard remained a deep, soft emerald. Stubborn and lush. Edwin had always said the verdure was a sign of God's love, a beautiful thing to gladden the hearts of the mourning.

Mother Ardith had said it was because so many corpses made for good soil.

Tate pressed her hand to Edwin's name stone. Mother Ardith's name stone was just to the side—the last name stone they'd been able to make before the mason had left to fight the Normans—and behind Tate was a row of fresh graves, marked with slabs of wood clumsily carved with crosses.

The graveyard would have very good soil indeed before this was through.

"Tate," a familiar voice said. "There's something you should see."

Tate stood and brushed off her habit. She turned to see Wynflaed standing near the row of new graves, pale face drawn under her veil. Tate had already known it couldn't be good news—there had been no good news since William the Bastard first arrived on their shores nearly two years ago—but if it was enough to upset the typically sweet-natured Wynflaed, it had to be bad even by their new standards.

"Of course," she told her friend. She gave one last look at Edwin and Mother Ardith's graves—their chaplain and their abbess, both in the ground far too soon—and took in a steadying breath. "Take me there."

* * *

The smoke on the horizon was no more than a smudge when they climbed out of the valley that sheltered Far Hope Abbey, but it was undeniably smoke. It met a pale, cloudless sky and then faded into the blue. It came from some miles away; the village of Sutreworde if Tate had to guess.

Half a day's ride away. Less with good horses.

The Normans were coming. And if Tate had prayed the abbey would be spared on account of its remoteness, its isolation from anything to do with politics or war, then her prayers hadn't been answered.

"It's because of Gytha's rebellion in Exeter," Wynflaed said. "It's drawn the new king's ire."

Gytha Thorkelsdóttir was the mother of the defeated, and now very dead, King Harold, who'd been shot through the eye...or hacked to pieces...or some other manner of horrible death at the Battle of Hastings. The rumor was that Gytha had begun planning her rebellion the minute William had taken the field, sending her grandsons to Ireland to raise an army and then join her here in Devon to defeat the bastard king at last.

And so the Normans who'd been mostly preoccupied with establishing power around London and in the north had turned their gaze to the West Country. And it was a gaze without mercy or quarter.

Tate stood watching the smoke for a minute more, the cold spring wind whipping her veil around her shoulders. "It is death to stay in their path," she said finally. She turned to Wynflaed. "You need to leave."

Wynflaed's pretty face set in a mulish expression. "No. I'm not leaving you. And I'm not leaving Far Hope."

Tate looked down to the valley where their abbey nestled between the hills. At the site of their holy spring stood several stone buildings with arched windows filled with glass, their insides draped in gold cloth and vibrant hangings. Far Hope Abbey was a wealthy place and therefore a ripe target for plunder. Apparently a century or so of Christianity hadn't been enough to shake the Normans of their ancestral urge to pillage. It had happened to churches and monasteries all over England since Hastings, and now it was going to happen to Far Hope.

Tate wasn't giving up Far Hope without a fight. But she also wasn't going to risk the lives of her sisters and the abbey's pilgrims; she needed everyone who was physically capable of fleeing to do so.

"Wynflaed," Tate said as gently as she could, because she wasn't a gentle person by nature. "Take the rest of the sisters and the pilgrims to my brother's house. You're the only one here besides me who knows the way, and Thornchurch will be safe from raids—or suspicion."

Tate's brother, Heorot, had already sworn fealty to William, had done it the moment he saw the tide turn at Hastings. He'd gone to Sussex to fight for King Harold and had surrendered on the field instead, pledging his loyalty to William and then staying for the foreign duke's disastrous coronation in London. William had rewarded Heorot by allowing him to keep his lands. Heorot was one of the few English thegns allowed to do so.

Wynflaed looked southeast, in the direction of Thornchurch and its small village of Thorncombe. "It's a long way," she said uncertainly, and Tate gave her a tight smile.

"And it's a short way to heaven if you don't leave," she said. "Only the distance of a Norman arrow. Please, Wynflaed. I'll lock the gates after you, and it will hold them out for some time. God willing, a few weeks. But I'll last much longer with less mouths to feed."

Wynflaed looked troubled but couldn't argue with Tate. She knew Tate was right. "It just doesn't seem fair," she said softly, taking her friend's hand. "That you have to stay while the rest of us flee to safety."

"I'm the abbess," Tate said, and after six months, it still felt strange to say. Wrong to say. Abbesses were supposed to be experienced, good of spirit, well past the bloom of youth. Tate was only twenty-five years old, and not a bit good of spirit. She'd come to Far Hope to atone, after all, to serve the penance she owed God. She hadn't come to Far Hope because she wanted status or advancement.

But there were only a handful of nuns left now at Far Hope, which had already been a small place before the war, and it had lost too many sisters since the Normans had come. Novices running back home to families that needed them, sickness claiming Mother Ardith, along with so many others...

So when it came time to select a new abbess, Tate was the only fully vowed nun who was also in good enough health for the job. And after being elected by her few remaining sisters, Tate had gone to her room and wept—but she'd also promised herself after her tears had dried that she would never curse her fate again. Her sisters deserved better. Far Hope deserved better.

She didn't rail or cry now when it meant that she must stay to face the Normans. It was her responsibility, her duty.

And her penance would have to wait.

"Come," Tate said, touching her friend's shoulder. Wynflaed looked surprised; Tate wasn't normally affectionate, hadn't been since before she came to the abbey. In those earlier years, she had felt she didn't deserve affection or comfort, and it had become a habit she couldn't break. "I'll help you prepare."

They went down the hidden path from the hills into the sheltered valley below, and Tate dispatched Wynflaed to organize provisions. She would take the last of the asses and carts with her to Thornchurch, carrying the sisters and pilgrims who were too infirm to walk, and they would cache some of Far Hope's treasures inside.

Heorot would keep them safe for as long as he could. He was a loyal brother and a good man, and anyone raised at Thornchurch understood the need for keeping old things safe and secret.

As they were packing the carts, a horse thundered through the gates, its rider covered in sweat despite the late winter day. It was Seamere, a beekeeper from two villages over.

"It's the Wolf," he panted, not bothering to get down from his horse. "At Sutreworde. I just heard from the miller of Ashburton, who heard from someone in Bovey. The Wolf is coming this way."

Tate stopped packing the cart—mostly linens and wool blankets, along with several skins of water to last the caravan the half-day journey. She was surprised to see her hands were shaking.

She spoke softly to make sure that her voice didn't tremble as well. "Are you sure?"

Seamere nodded. "The miller was certain it's him. They're saying that William the Bastard has given him free rein to sack as much as Devon as he pleases until the rebels at Exeter surrender."

God damn Gytha and her stubbornness! It was one thing to bring the king's attention to an already beleaguered land, but for *the Wolf* to be unleashed upon them merely for her stupid scheme to set one of her hapless grandsons at the opposite end of a battlefield from William...it was absurdity. Selfish absurdity. William might be cruel, tyrannical, a threat to Tate's beloved English church, but one thing he was not was a bad commander. He would win this fight and he would keep on winning every fight after, because God had forsaken this land and the people in it.

All that was left to do was protect the few blessings remaining. Like Far Hope.

"Did you say the Wolf?" Leofgifu asked. She was a resident at the abbey, an earl's widowed niece who hadn't wanted to remarry and also hadn't wanted to take the veil. She would stay with Tate to help with the few pilgrims and sisters who couldn't make the journey to Thornchurch even by cart, and as much as Tate wanted her to go, Leofgifu was their most skilled healer. The remaining pilgrims couldn't spare her. "But I thought he went back to Normandy. After..."

She didn't have to finish for Tate and Seamere to take her meaning. They all knew what the *after* meant.

After the Wolf had cut a swath of burning, pillaging destruction from Hastings to Southwark, and then all the way to Oxford.

After his name had become a byword for Norman terror.

"There's no way he won't come here to the abbey," Seamere said. He looked apologetic. "All of you should leave, as quickly as you can."

If only it were that easy. Tate didn't waste her time arguing with him, though. Only she and a few other people knew Far Hope's secrets, and even now, about to face down a horde of Normans, she would die for those secrets. She would keep them safe.

"You have others to warn," Tate said to Seamere. "We won't keep you."

He looked torn. "If I could stay to fight, I would—"

"You're better off telling everyone you can. Maybe there's still time to bury their valuables. There's certainly still time to flee." Tate looked at the sky. Twilight crept in early, the last gloomy vestige of winter, and she estimated they had three or so hours of safety left, depending on how thoroughly the riders would ransack Ashburton and Houndtor on their way here. So long as she could get the sisters and pilgrims on their way to Thornchurch in the next hour, they'd be well off the road the Normans would take into the valley.

She hoped.

Seamere gave her and Leofgifu a reluctant nod. He was a pious man, and he wouldn't like the thought of leaving nuns and pilgrims to face the Normans on their own. But Tate gave him her most serene smile, the one she'd seen Mother Ardith give well-meaning and ill-meaning men alike. On her, it probably looked more like a strained frown, but it seemed to do the job.

"God will keep you safe," Seamere said, clearly believing it, and then he wheeled off.

Tate wanted to laugh. God hadn't kept a single English person safe in two years.

There was no reason he would start now.

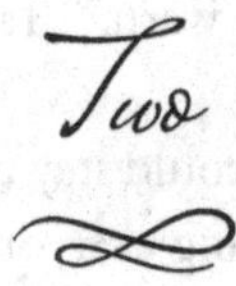

TATE

THE NORMANS DIDN'T COME.

All that evening, past vespers and into compline, Tate waited.

And as the moon rose, Tate waited.

She waited as she and Leofgifu and Judith—a sister who had a demon which tormented her with a terror of leaving the abbey walls—tended to their eldest sisters and the two remaining pilgrims. And before she'd allow herself even the *hope* that they might make it through the night without the Normans reaching their gates, she took the twisting path out of the valley and up the hills and then searched the dark horizon.

And there she waited too.

Sutreworde still burned, judging from the red-orange glow on the horizon, but Tate could make out nothing else. No torches, no dark shadows resolving themselves into riders on the road. People talked about the Wolf as if he were magic, a demon, something more than human, but Tate was too practical for all that. She knew that he had to move and attack as a normal man would.

Mother Ardith, too, had scoffed whenever she heard people spinning each other into a panic about the Wolf's uncanny ability to strike villages and churches unawares.

As if being Norman weren't bad enough, she'd said. *He doesn't need to be magic if he's clever, and he doesn't need to be a demon if he's greedy. Ordinary human evil will do the rest.*

Tate tended to agree. People would be surprised at the evil ordinary people were capable of, even people who seemed normal and good and innocent. There didn't need to be a supernatural reason for violence. Or murder.

Tate knew that truth intimately, thoroughly. She traced its shape at night with her thoughts; it covered her face like a shroud while she slept.

It crouched over her constantly, the lid to a coffin only she could see.

The good news was that Far Hope was safe from demons and ordinary men alike, hidden in its valley as it was. Steep hills sheltered it on three sides, and the way into the abbey was shielded with high walls and a thick wooden gate. The abbey had a good spring and plenty of provisions, and for those reasons, Tate could hold Far Hope for a while, at least. The Normans would have to get through the gate, which would take time to arrange, and they'd need tunnels to breach the walls, which would take time to dig.

There was the private way down to the back of the abbey from the moors, of course, but it was hidden with rocks and heather, and too steep for horses or anyone carrying heavy weapons—or wearing mail shirts. Even if the Normans did find it, they'd have to tether their horses, strip off their weapons and armor, and make their way down one by one. Hardly the way to keep speed and surprise on their side.

What Tate would do before the Normans breached the

walls or starved them out, she didn't know. She supposed she would try to negotiate, or maybe she could pay them off with the few treasures that weren't currently trundling their way to her childhood home. But damn it all, she'd been trusted with Far Hope, however mistakenly, and she would defend it with everything she had.

Tate went back down to the dormitory, thinking of the last conversation she had with her mentor before the old abbess had died.

It can't be me, she'd whispered to Mother Ardith as her abbess lay dying on a pallet stuffed with dried herbs and flowers to freshen the room. *It can't be me.*

Daughter, whyever not?

You know why. You know what I've done. I'm here for penance, nothing more.

A wet, wheezing laugh. *If you don't think leadership is penance, then you have much still to learn.*

And now Tate could see what Mother Ardith meant. It was up to Tate to keep the abbey and the people inside it safe by any means possible. No matter the cost.

And with the Wolf practically at her door, she had to consider that any cost might be necessary.

* * *

There'd been no sign of the Normans long after the world had gone dark, and so Tate had allowed herself a few hours of sleep before matins. The sleep was fitful, fretful, and filled with half-dreams of the Wolf. A giant man, she was sure, on account of the Viking blood in his veins. And he looked like a monster, that was certain. He couldn't look otherwise with the tales they told about him.

In her dreams, she saw every village he'd slaughtered, every house he'd burned. Every drop of blood dripping from the edge of the axe they said he favored. And when she woke up, blinking in the dark, her breath lodged in her chest like it was stuck there with glue, she knew he was here.

She just *knew*.

She rolled off her pallet and slipped into her soft leather shoes, and then crept out of her cell. Their dormitory was made of only a few rooms, and typically she shared her cell with Wynflaed and four other sisters, but they were gone now, and so she didn't worry about waking anyone as she slung her mantle over her shoulders and stepped into the chilly night.

The stars glittered overhead, but she barely noticed because there were dozens of tiny suns burning outside the wall guarding the abbey from the rest of the valley. They disappeared from view as she drew closer to the wall, but she found the chink between the gate and the stone and then caught her breath.

Yes, those were torches and fires. Close enough that she could see the small, pale hillocks of the tents, but far enough away that she couldn't count the men or the horses. They must have come quietly. Silently. She would have thought that impossible for any band of soldiers, much less ones known for rapaciousness and marauding.

"I didn't hear them at first," Leofgifu said quietly from next to her.

Tate didn't turn. "Nor I."

"Why have they made camp?" Leofgifu asked. "Surely it would have been better to catch us unawares."

"Maybe they didn't know about our wall and wanted to wait until daytime to search for its weaknesses. Or maybe they were tired from a long day of looting, and they know we're not exactly going to fortify ourselves while they rest." Tate closed her eyes and tried to think how Mother Ardith would think. The trouble was that her own thoughts—her own *feelings*, the ones she'd come to Far Hope to escape—were so *loud*. She was furious, hopeless, terrified. She wanted to scream, to cry, to fight.

God help her, she even wanted to run.

"At least we know they're here now," observed Leofgifu. "They can't surprise us."

Surprise.

A very stupid idea occurred to Tate.

She looked at Leofgifu and then back at Far Hope, its stone structures as solid as the moors, as fixed to this place as the hills.

If you don't think leadership is penance, then you have much left to learn.

Tate took a breath. "I'm going to their camp. Now."

"*What?*" Leofgifu looked aghast. "Tate, you cannot. You know you cannot. They might hold you for ransom. Or they might kill you! They might…"

She didn't finish her sentence, but neither did she have to. They both knew what invaders did. What the Normans had done, and the Vikings before them, and even the Saxons before them. On and on until one got back to the books of Deuteronomy and Numbers.

"I know what they might do," Tate said firmly. "But neither can I sit here and wait for them to decide. The Wolf is but a Norman, after all. If I can't trade on his devotion to God, then perhaps I can trade on his greed."

And perhaps, she didn't add, *I can trade on other things.* Whatever sin she might have to commit to keep her abbey safe, it was a far worse sin to do nothing. God would forgive her. And if he didn't?

Well, then, she was already quite used to that.

* * *

Leofgifu didn't like it one bit, but she helped Tate dress properly in her habit and wimple, and then draw her heaviest mantle over it all. She didn't take any kind of light with her, although even she struggled on the moors when it was full dark. But they were only a few hours from dawn, and if she did get lost, it wouldn't last long.

After Leofgifu promised to take care of the others and charge Judith with leading prayers in Tate's absence, Tate took the path from behind the abbey up to the moors. It twisted up the hills surrounding Far Hope and then ended near a cluster of granite boulders, which were only visible by the way they blotted out part of the sky as one approached. Tate could now look down the length of the Hope Valley and see the single burning light in the abbey dormitory, and then, past the walls, the small lake of torches belonging to the Normans.

It wasn't easy to stay quiet when the path was a sheep trail through the heather, and also when she couldn't see, but she did a commendable job as she walked along the lip of the valley until she was above the camp itself. She counted fifteen tents but many more horses, and saw two guards at either side of the camp—two facing the abbey, two facing the rest of the valley. None facing the hills. And why would they? They were far from any settlement that could give them real trouble, and there were no English soldiers left to chase them off. They were all either sworn to William, or sworn to people who'd sworn to William, or dead.

Besides, the steep talus of the valley wall didn't make for an easy vector of attack. It was the kind of slope that accommodated gnarled twists of heather, stubborn moss, and little else. Even Tate, short, slight, and unencumbered as she was, nearly tumbled to her death a few times.

But finally, she made it, and she paused just outside the glow of the flickering torches and tried to remember how to breathe. She could see piles of weapons inside some of the tents—quivers full of arrow shafts as thick as thumbs, swords as tall as she was. And all around the fires were the sleeping forms of soldiers, long and massive. Far Hope saw plenty of men—priests and pilgrims and the occasional monk—but none of them were *soldiers*. None of them looked like they could snap Tate in half with their bare hands.

Stepping into this camp was beyond foolish; it was practically begging for death.

Which I'm sure many of the Wolf's victims did before he finally let them die.

That was not going to happen to anyone inside Far Hope, and with that thought, Tate set her shoulders and lifted her chin the way she'd seen Mother Ardith do when they were visited by princes and kings. Like they had no authority over her, the keeper of a secret older than Rome itself.

And then Tate walked into the camp.

She strode over to one of the guards facing the abbey, who was huffing and shifting his feet dramatically as if he'd never been this cold before in his life, and she tapped him on the shoulder.

He jumped like Jacob's angel himself had come down to wrestle him, and his partner spun around, drawing his sword and his dagger at the same time. But then the hand holding the dagger dropped a little.

"No camp followers," the guard said shortly in Norman French. "Go back home."

Tate flashed him a look that made him shut his mouth.

"I'm here for the Wolf," she said, also in Norman, her voice as cool as the night around them. "Not coin."

The first guard laughed. *Laughed.* Oh, that pissed Tate right off.

"The Wolf isn't taking *guests* right now," he told her, his clean-shaven face in an ugly smirk.

"I'm not here for pleasure," Tate said. "I'm the abbess of the abbey you're about to pillage."

Another laugh. "And I'm the princess of Bohemia. Fuck off."

Tate had known this since she was sixteen, but she learned it all over again in that moment: Sometimes, fear felt like courage. Sometimes it didn't even feel like fear at all, but cold, bright fury.

"I *will* see the Wolf," she said calmly, "either with your escort or without it. One way will displease him more, I'm sure."

"Not if we tie up those pretty praying hands and keep you right here with us," the second guard said. He didn't lift his dagger, but Tate saw his grip shift.

She made herself shrug, like it made no difference to her. "Then I'll scream and the Wolf will hear, and I'll have my audience."

They didn't seem to like that option either—probably judging it better to wake the Wolf with a request rather than a scream splitting the night. They gave each other a look.

"Come on then," the first one said gruffly, taking her by the arm through her mantle. "Let's get you what you came for. Much though you may regret it."

They walked to a tent in the middle of the camp. The flap was down, but a small brazier clearly burned inside, and Tate could hear the *shing-shiiiing* of metal against stone. Like a weapon being carefully, methodically sharpened.

The Wolf was awake.

The guard hadn't even tugged the flap aside when an irritable voice from within said in Norman, "Can I not get a moment's rest?"

Tate could not have said what voice she'd expected the Wolf to have, precisely, only that it was not this one. Rich and husky. Pitched lower than hers, but still not a voice that Tate would hear and ascribe to a legendary soldier.

Or even to a man at all.

"Apologies," the guard said, sounding truly contrite. And a little afraid. "But there is someone here. She says she is the abbess of Far Hope."

There was movement inside the tent, and then the flap twitched aside. The Wolf stepped out into the night, illuminated by a torch set outside the tent and the brazier from behind. And despite the whispers and tales, the Wolf was not a monster at all.

There was pale, freckled skin and hair partially braided back in small plaits that then came down to mingle in the Wolf's loose strawberry tresses. There was a full pink mouth and gold eyes; there were cheekbones as high as the Devonshire sky and a jaw as finely wrought as the gold and enamel crosses inside the abbey.

The Wolf was beautiful, and Tate felt her heart tumble abruptly inside her chest.

"You're the Wolf," Tate said, mostly to herself, and the Wolf regarded her with a piercing, cool gaze.

"I am."

"You're—you're not..."

"A man?" the Wolf asked in Norman-accented English. She turned to go back inside the tent, gesturing for the guards to bring Tate in after her. "You *are* very deep in the hinterlands, aren't you?" she asked over her shoulder. "The east and south of your country know me well enough. Adelais of the Maine, at your pleasure."

Tate shuffled unthinkingly into the tent behind the warrior, her mind recalibrating to this new information.

Adelais of the Maine.

In every story she'd heard, the Wolf had been a man, a vicious, murdering *he*. But every story she'd heard had passed through many mouths before it had been spoken to her—and in any event, who would believe this without seeing it with their own eyes? That William's most terrifying warrior was a woman so beautiful she put literal treasures to shame?

"Leave us," Adelais said to her guards in Norman. "And do not disturb me for any reason. I want the abbess all to myself."

Three

THE WOLF

ADELAIS of the Maine had never enjoyed being the Wolf as much as she did in this moment.

The abbess stepped backward now, practically falling onto the low cot at the back of the tent, her green eyes wide as she stared at Adelais. As she caught her balance, Adelais smiled at her—a smile she knew had made grown men piss themselves —and then she sat on the stool a few paces away.

Either the abbess would have to stand while Adelais sat, or she'd have to sit on Adelais's cot, which meant she'd have to look up at Adelais while they spoke. Either way put her at a disadvantage, and Adelais could see that the abbess understood this too. But to Adelais's surprise—and pleasure—the abbess didn't hesitate. She sat on the neatly made cot, her shoulders lifting ever so slightly under her mantle.

A deep breath.

She was nervous. Or scared.

Adelais's smile grew even wider.

"How old are you?" she murmured in her own tongue,

more to herself than to her unexpected guest. She spread her feet and reached for the axe she'd been sharpening before she'd been interrupted. It was plenty sharp already, but she liked the way the little nun's eyes warily traced the edge. Adelais felt like a cat watching a very pretty mouse.

"Twenty-five," the nun answered in flawless Norman.

Fascinating. Adelais had met a handful of diplomats and courtiers with passable Norman—since the reign of Aethelred, the English court had been connected by marriage to Normandy, with plenty of family and trade ties knotting the two shores together—but it was remarkable to find someone so far from London or Canterbury able to speak it fluently.

It was also fascinating that the nun hadn't elaborated on her unusual age for such a high station. Granted, Adelais was mostly among soldiers and warriors, but it still struck her as strange that her visitor didn't boast about reaching such a position while being so young. As a greener woman, Adelais might have chalked it up to this person being in the church and therefore humble, but she knew better now. Holy people put soldiers and kings to shame with the tales they told about themselves and their calling from God.

But she also remembered what the archbishop had called the abbess when telling her about the abbey. *Tate the Pious.*

Perhaps that piety was real. Adelais couldn't decide what interested her more: the idea that this lovely flower before her was truly saintly, or that she'd somehow fooled the entire West Country into thinking she was.

"Twenty-five is young for your position."

"It's uncommon for someone my age to be an abbess, yes," the nun acknowledged.

Indeed. "Let's be direct, Mother Tate," Adelais said, thoroughly enjoying the surprise flitting across the nun's face as she realized that Adelais knew her name. "What did you come to offer me not to break down your abbey walls and burn everything I find?"

Tate's gaze was level, direct. There was no cowering; neither was there any bluster. Which made her rise a few notches in Adelais's estimation. It was a rare thing to find someone willing to trade in objective truths with Adelais's axe between them.

"I can offer you prayers," Tate said.

"Prayers are cheap," mused Adelais. "What about masses instead?"

The abbess didn't reveal anything by expression or posture, but that itself was revealing enough. "We are currently without a chaplain," she said. There was a careful neutrality to her voice when she said the word *chaplain*, almost as if she were trying to compensate for an internal lack of calm. "But once we have one restored to the abbey, then yes, I could promise you masses."

Adelais set the axe down on the thin carpet rolled over the grass, the double-edged head planted between her feet. She leaned forward over the handle as if to tell the abbess a secret. "You *could* promise them, but unfortunately for you, I don't require them. My late husband already commissioned masses for his soul and mine before his death."

Tate nodded, once and a little crisply. Her composure now was interesting to Adelais, especially contrasted with the deep breaths and the wide eyes earlier. It wasn't sangfroid, not really, but the calmness mingled with the agitation beneath made Adelais want to see how deep the control ran. Most people were cowards, and it was hard to believe that an abbess in the middle of nowhere would have more courage than King Harold's soldiers defending their home from Adelais's men. But the possibility of being surprised was even better than the possibility of a good fight, and Adelais leaned back, mind filling with very delightful ideas about how to provoke this woman further.

"Far Hope has some valuables," said Tate. She spoke so calmly and steadily that Adelais suspected that this was what the abbess had really come to offer: a sort of modernized version of the Danegeld. Pay off the raider with some of what they'd planned to steal, saving time and bloodshed for everyone.

Adelais *had* come to raid the abbey, that part was true. But she'd come to Far Hope for two reasons, and only one of them had to do with helping herself to Far Hope's treasures. And even then, she wasn't interested in the offering box or the church silverware.

She'd heard the name of Far Hope long before she'd come to England, as a girl of ten at her father's side. They'd traveled from Angers to the court of Henri for yet another interminable visit having to do with their province, Maine, being squabbled over by Normandy, and Blois, and the Angevins. Adelais had never cared much for politics unless it meant fighting later, but she did like games, and sometimes politicking was like a game. However, there was one thing she liked even more than games, and that was a secret.

Late one night, when everyone but her father and the king were asleep, she'd heard them whispering. She'd been allowed to stay near her father, curled behind his chair on a thick blanket, partly because he was fond of his fierce little daughter—his only child and the one into whom he poured all the martial aspirations he'd stored up for a son that never came—and partly because tensions around Maine were high enough that a viscount's child was at risk of being taken and held hostage as leverage somewhere. He didn't let her out of his sight whenever they left home.

They'd thought she'd been asleep as they started talking of

a place in England, a place the king had been to visit—secretly —the year before.

The spies say King Edward goes three times a year, her father had murmured.

I do not blame him. I would go again if I felt I could leave Paris and not come back to my brother trying to steal it, the French king had said. *It is the greatest ecstasy I have ever known, what I found at Far Hope.*

Her father had paused, and then had said with the casual inflection of someone trying not to sound too interested. *What did you find there?*

The king had not answered right away, and when he finally did answer, his voice hadn't sounded devout, or even joyful. But almost haunted.

They keep old ways at Far Hope, you must understand. And a treasure even the pope himself could only ever wish to see.

A treasure even greater than what the pope had? In the Holy City itself? A treasure so great that a king spoke of it with more emotion in his voice than when he spoke of his own crown?

Adelais's kin were a hundred years removed from being pillagers and raiders, having adapted quickly to the territorial land warfare that dominated France, becoming a people of castles, horses, farms. It was a shame in Adelais's mind because she wanted nothing more than to be a shield-maiden, sailing off to far-flung shores for loot and glory.

And so when she heard of this treasure, her whole being had come alive with light and color, like the sun shining through a stained glass window.

Far Hope. The English name had stuck in her mind, engraved itself. *Far Hope*. Her pagan ancestors had raided Lindisfarne and Iona, every vulnerable holy place they could find, and though Rollo's people were all Christian now, it didn't dim Adelais's urge to go there and snatch this treasure for herself.

And when she'd come to England eighteen years later, as part of William's attempt to seize his stolen crown, she knew it was her destiny to go to Far Hope and find this treasure at last. It had taken a not-insignificant number of sly threats to squeeze more information out of Stigand, England's corrupt archbishop, but she eventually learned the abbey was in Devonshire, hidden in the hills near an ancient wood. From there, she'd only needed a reason to come to the West Country —which the Exeter rebels had so handily provided—and for the locals to tell her which roads to take. Wild, rough roads that she was surprised King Henri would have deigned to use.

But perhaps for a treasure without compare, any road was worth taking.

Here in the tent, Adelais studied the young abbess, who sat as still as one of the granite tors standing sentinel in the hills. Immutable, rooted so deep that only lifetimes of wind and rain could hope to shift it, bit by invisible bit.

She was small, which Adelais had noticed right away, used to gauging how much of a fight a person would put up if pressed to it. And she was not only slender in a way that suggested prayerful fasting and abnegation, but she was short, barely coming to Adelais's shoulder. Adelais was a tall woman, another gift from her Northman ancestors, but Tate would be diminutive by anyone's standards.

And while Tate was strangely pretty, she wasn't beautiful. Not beautiful like people said Adelais herself was. The nun had forgettable brown hair, dark brows which were thick and straight, and elfin features. Delicate but too grave for loveliness.

Despite that, Adelais found her gaze drawn again and again to the holy woman's lips. It wasn't a lush mouth, not the kind of mouth you'd look for in a mistress, say, but it had the most fascinating downward curve to it whenever the abbess let her mask slip. As if someone born to pout had been made to frown instead.

Adelais wondered what it would look like in its natural shape—or in a gasp. She even wondered what it might look like in a *smile*, which was unusual. She didn't often find herself caring if someone smiled or not, with the two exceptions of her father, when he'd been alive, and her son, now a young man being fostered in Caen.

But there it was: She wanted to see this abbess smile.

More typically, she'd also like to see Tate's mouth swollen, panting, wet. But Adelais set that aside for the moment.

"I have plenty of valuables already," Adelais told the nun frankly. Her husband Gérald had been a wealthy castellan of William's and a favored warrior, and her own dowry had been substantial.

And she'd pleased William enough with her marauding that he was planning to gift her with estates here in England as a reward—in her son's name, of course. Because while William was happy enough for her to be his pet Amazon, his kept nightmare with which to torment the English, some walls were unbreachable. She could be William's tool, a story meant to strike terror into the hearts of his conquered people, and she could murder and pillage on his behalf.

But she could not have a house in her own right, even though it wasn't that uncommon in this new English land of theirs.

"I don't need coins and candlesticks," Adelais continued. "Come on, little nun, what else can you offer me?"

A flush spread anew over Tate's cheeks, and Adelais tilted her head. She wanted the abbess to speak of the *treasure*, the one that had so thoroughly haunted the king. But now the abbess almost looked—well, Adelais wasn't entirely sure what to make of that look. It could have been embarrassment, or it could have been nervousness.

But there was something *secret*-like in the way the abbess dipped her gaze and swallowed. And ah, how Adelais loved secrets.

"I'm aware there is more to plundering than taking gold, and I would offer it freely. Only myself, though. The other sisters would stay untouched."

As in a good fight, Adelais's body knew the answer before her mind, and heat pooled in her belly. "So it's true what they say about the English church," Adelais said, her voice a little huskier now. "Merry monks and married priests. A shame the Wolf is not what you expected, for it would have been a very pretty offer."

The abbess met her stare, her eyes shining in the light of brazier. "You misunderstand me. I'm still offering it."

A log in the brazier popped, and the wind nipped at the flap of the tent. Adelais couldn't tear her eyes away from the woman in front of her, couldn't stop staring at the fascinating little elf with her plain habit and her mouth made for pouting. Adelais felt for a moment like she had as a girl on King Henri's floor hearing about Far Hope for the first time: filled with light and color and curiosity. Filled with a bright, sharp hunger.

"You're offering to fuck me," Adelais said bluntly, meaning to shock the abbess perhaps, but also needing to be sure. Because abruptly, she couldn't think of anything that wasn't having Tate squirming underneath her.

If Adelais had offended her, Tate didn't show it. "Yes," she said. "One night, and then you'll leave."

Adelais could have laughed. Here was the most interesting creature Adelais had ever found—here was the most fun that she'd had in years *and* the seat of twenty years' worth of curiosity—and this sweet nun thought one night would be payment enough to send her away for good.

"But I don't want to leave," Adelais said with a wolfish smile. "So you're going to have to do better than that."

Tate briefly rolled her lips inward, took a breath. "Two nights."

"Even two *very good* nights are not that much payment, little mouse. I can find two good nights anywhere in the kingdom." In fact, her last lay, a barmaid in Langport, had been one of the finest fucks she'd had—and that included Adelais's late husband, who, despite being a vainglorious prick, had been incredible in bed. "How about this—for every night you give me, I shall grant you a day's worth of reprieve, and I won't attack your abbey."

Tate's dark brows lifted. "What, in perpetuity? Am I to pleasure you for the rest of our earthly lives?"

"Don't tempt me, mouse." She was still smiling, but she knew Tate could hear the danger in Adelais's voice by the way she tensed. "I have half a mind to carry you off like I would a bag of candlesticks as it is. But I want what's inside this abbey too badly to leave it."

Tate seemed to regain control. "It's an abbey like any other."

"So the pious women here lie as well as fuck," observed Adelais. "Because I've known there is a secret here at Far Hope since I was a child. A treasure. And I want it. I want whatever brings princes and kings here to behold."

Tate's lips parted. Closed. When she spoke, her words were careful. "Those are ordinary pilgrimages. To pray near our relics and see our holy spring."

"Bullshit," Adelais cut in. "You think Henri couldn't find a pilgrimage to make in France or that your King Edward wouldn't have been satisfied by making a pilgrimage somewhere more convenient than an abbey in the middle of a vast and weathered nowhere? You're telling me that whatever saint's knucklebone you have in your church is more important than any other saint's chunk of rib or bitten-off fingernail? I know there's something here, Tate, and I want it. I've wanted it for twenty years."

"It can't be stolen," Tate replied, lifting her chin.

Can't be stolen.

Not that it shouldn't be; not that it would be wrong to steal it. But *can't*.

Interesting.

"How about a little game, then?" Adelais said, leaning over her axe once more. "A bet, if you will."

"A bet," Tate repeated.

"You fuck me for the next three nights, and I give you three days of peace. And if I cannot learn what I want by then, I will leave."

Tate's eyebrow lifted the slightest amount. "That's it? Three nights and you will leave?"

"*If* I don't learn the secrets of this place."

"You would only learn them from me, and you must know that I will never tell you," Tate said plainly. "This seems like a step back in your negotiations."

Adelais shrugged. It would hardly help her agenda to explain to Tate why it wasn't.

Tate seemed to suspect a trap, searching Adelais's face with an intensity that pleased Adelais. She liked having Tate's attention. She wanted more of it.

All of it.

Tate looked down at her hands as if thinking, and then finally nodded. "Yes. Yes, we have an agreement. Three nights in your bed, and if you cannot learn what you want to know, then you'll leave."

"And if I do learn..." Adelais smiled again. "Then I'm taking it."

Tate's mouth flickered with something that could have been a smile. "You could try."

Adelais laughed. "I'll teach you not to doubt me, sweet thing. Now," she said, placing her axe on the floor behind her and reaching for the ties at her waist. She needed that strange, pretty mouth between her legs like she needed to draw breath. "Let's get started, shall we?"

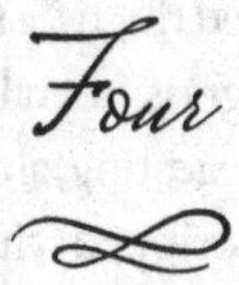

TATE

SHE MISSED Edwin more than ever now. Because one day she was going to have to confess something deeply ugly, and it was this: She was burning alive at the sight of Adelais's hands deftly working open the knots of her braies.

Tate had seen plenty of nakedness in her life and was no stranger to it at Far Hope, but the revelation of the Wolf's creamy hips and thighs, the seam of her pussy clothed with silky red curls...they stole the thoughts from Tate's mind. She suddenly couldn't remember why she was here, what she'd left behind Far Hope's walls, why she should do this only as an exchange, only for Far Hope's benefit.

All she could think of was the Wolf. Adelais.

All she could think of was the wet warmth pulling at her own sex, begging for her to rub it, please it.

With her braies and woolen chausses off, Adelais pushed her tunic up to her waist and once again spread her legs. Her cunt awaited, glistening in the brazier light. She was wet already.

"Come here," she ordered with arrogance of someone who was rarely refused, and Tate slid off the cot to her knees, crawled the few feet over to her abbey's would-be invader, and knelt between Adelais's planted feet. This close, she could see a few lone freckles on Adelais's muscled thighs, a faded scar on the outside of her hip. She smelled like grass, metal, and sweat, but it wasn't unpleasant at all. It was intoxicating, almost. The smell of a soldier.

Adelais impatiently stripped the wimple and veil from Tate's hair, and then her right hand molded tight to the shape of Tate's head after the fabric was tossed aside. Tate could feel the restrained strength in that hand as it pushed her closer to where she was wanted, and a strange happiness swam in her veins. She couldn't say why—or even *what* that happiness was —only that it was a ticklish, burning sort of joy as Adelais held Tate by the hair and forced her to her cunt.

Forced was the wrong word, maybe, because Tate had offered and agreed. She'd chosen to do it.

But after having chosen, the feeling of being made to do this was...overwhelming. Breathtaking. Tate could hardly think as she kissed the soft split between Adelais's thighs, and her body keened for sex as she'd never felt it keen before. She'd done so much at Far Hope, and yet she'd never done *this*, whatever this was. This wicked bargaining, this near-coercion.

Adelais seemed to like it too, forcing Tate's mouth even harder against her until Tate parted her lips and gave Adelais her tongue, which made the warrior grunt and push her hips into Tate's mouth.

"More," ordered Adelais, using the hand on Tate's head to move her up and down. Tate flattened her tongue and allowed Adelais to fuck her swollen clitoris against it for a long moment, Adelais's breaths coming deep and steady as she did.

Tate fluttered her tongue, pushing back against Adelais's hold to flick the tip of her tongue against the stiff bud, and

Adelais groaned and pushed Tate's head back in again. "You're good at this. So goddamn good."

Tate knew it; she'd had enough practice at Far Hope, after all.

"Suck it," the Wolf said roughly now. "I want to come."

Tate panted against Adelais's wet, sweet skin, a bolt of lust arrowing through her body straight to her own pussy, and she nearly couldn't *exist* for it, she couldn't imagine anything other than this, and she never wanted to. She sealed her lips around the tight bud and sucked and was rewarded with another buck of Adelais's hips. The warrior hissed with pleasure, her hand even tighter in Tate's hair.

"That's it," muttered Adelais. "Just like that." But then she leaned forward and tore impatiently at Tate's mantle and then her habit. "Show me," she said. "I want to see your pretty tits."

Tate helped her pull off the habit, straightening up and sitting back on her heels while she pulled it over her head, and the first thing she saw once the fabric was free was the wild glow of Adelais's golden eyes.

"A nun has no business having a body like that," the Wolf said throatily, and then reached down to palm Tate's breasts, to weigh and squeeze them like fruit she wanted to buy. The peaks were tight and hard against the warrior's palms. "Show me your cunt now too."

Tate's entire being was fire and hunger as she obeyed, spreading her knees and leaning back so that her sex would be visible to Adelais's hot stare. What compelled her to do it, she couldn't say, but she slid her hand down the rise of her pubic bone and used two fingers to spread her labia apart so that Adelais could see her opening, so that Adelais could see how wet she was there.

Adelais went suddenly still, a predator scenting prey, her

eyes on Tate's open pussy. "Put your fingers in," Adelais said. "Show me what you look like filled up."

Tate was breathing so hard now that she could hardly hear anything over the rush of blood in her ears. The entire camp could have been marching around the tent in chain mail for all she knew, and yet she didn't care. She didn't care about anything except Adelais's rough words and doing something, anything, to ease this heavy ache between her legs.

She pushed two fingers into her hole, wet enough that she could glide right in. She pressed against her front walls until pleasure began thrumming through her stomach, but it wasn't satisfying. She needed more.

Adelais was watching her hungrily, and then without warning, she reached forward and seized Tate again, hauling her back to Adelais's waiting sex. Tate had to brace both her hands on Adelais's thighs for balance as Adelais speared her fingers into Tate's hair and crushed her mouth against Adelais's skin.

"I want your tongue in my hole," demanded Adelais. "Let me feel it."

Tate dutifully gave her tongue, finding Adelais's entrance and licking at its rim before pushing inside. Adelais was beyond wet now, and she tasted like honey and salt, like summer and the sea. Tate moaned faintly at the taste as Adelais fucked herself against her tongue and moaned again as Adelais reached down and roughly palmed one of Tate's naked breasts.

An image flitted through Tate's mind then. Of Adelais moving through the abbey at night, finding Tate alone in bed. Of a hand clapping over Tate's mouth while Adelais shoved up her skirts. Of a hard, unyielding hand between her legs.

Here in the tent, Tate's cunt pulsed. Her toes were curling in her boots.

In all the time she'd been at Far Hope, she'd never thought herself capable of wanting...that.

Someone finding her in the dark and holding her down.

Tate was squirming as Adelais dragged Tate's mouth back up to her clit and held her there, wishing she could reach down and push a hand between her legs. As it was, she was balanced with her hands on Adelais's thighs, and then Adelais took the hand that Tate had penetrated herself with and brought it up to her mouth. Tate had to fight not to fall forward.

She gasped as Adelais's tongue moved over the pads of her fingers, over the first knuckle and then under to the thin creases there. It was silky, tickling, soft. Tate felt every slide of it through her hand and up her arm, and down into her chest.

Adelais licked and sucked Tate's taste off her fingers like it was only thing she'd ever wanted, the only thing that could keep her alive. It was delicious and wonderful and so unexpectedly arousing to have her fingers sucked, that Tate nearly lost the rhythm of pleasuring the cunt in front of her. But Adelais made it easier, canting her hips up and keeping Tate's mouth exactly where she wanted it. And Tate sucked Adelais's clit exactly the same way she would a cock, with long, hollow-cheeked pulls and then dances of her tongue over the tiny tip that made Adelais's firm thighs tense around her.

"That's a very wicked mouth for such a pious woman," Adelais growled, dropping Tate's hand in order to grab a breast and squeeze. "Maybe that's what the kings visit for, hmm? A chance to feel that devout tongue all hot and pretty against their cocks?"

It was close enough to the truth that alarm skated through Tate's mind, but thankfully, Adelais was too busy fucking to connect the dots. She let go of Tate's breast, pushed both hands into Tate's now thoroughly mussed hair, and then climaxed with a loud grunt that the whole camp must have heard.

Adelais's hands were tight, her thighs locked, her breath

coming in one hard rush after another as her pussy clenched and loosened against Tate's mouth. Tate's chin was wet now, her scalp stinging, and she closed her eyes and wished it would never end. That Adelais would keep her here for days and fuck her mouth for every minute of it and eventually carry Tate off over her shoulder like she'd threatened earlier. As a captive, a spoil.

The thought was like a match to tinder, and Tate had the sudden terror that she would never, ever stop burning.

Adelais's pussy eventually stilled, but she held Tate there the entire time, as if to make sure she got every moment's use out of her. Finally, she slid her hands from Tate's hair, but as Tate straightened up and wiped her wet mouth with her forearm, Adelais made it clear they weren't done yet.

"Turn around," the Wolf ordered. "Hands and knees. Ass up."

Tate obeyed, entire body trembling, quivering. Naked, she could acutely feel where the air in the tent was warmed by the brazier and where it was cool from the night air seeping in from the cracks. She turned the way Adelais had indicated, with her back to the warrior, and then leaned over and rested her head on the thin carpet making the floor of the tent.

"Knees apart, abbess. I want to see you."

Tate moved her knees apart, cool air stroking her wet sex and moving over her exposed secret hole. Adelais grunted behind her, a satisfied noise.

"Make yourself come," she said. "Show me if those hands are as wicked as that mouth."

Tate whimpered into the carpet, already reaching back to rub her clit, shivering as she brushed against it with her fingers. It felt like it would burst if she touched it for real, but she couldn't *not* touch it, because if she didn't come, she'd die, her heart would stop and she'd die, the first person ever to die from not having an orgasm.

Tate grazed her clit once more and then she couldn't stop herself. Her hips were chasing her own touch, her hand couldn't move fast enough, hard enough, and it was beyond degrading to be like this, her legs spread and all her holes available to this warrior's gaze, bucking against her own hand like an animal because she'd been completely torn apart by lust.

But there was no other way, there was nothing else. There was only fucking and the memory of Adelais's hand in her hair and the image of that hand over her mouth in the dark, and then she came, wet and hard, her stomach cinching and her back arching and her thighs slamming together around her hand as she rode it for everything she was worth. The pleasure burned through her even faster than the lust had, searing up from her pussy to her chest, neck, face, scorching down her thighs to her calves and toes. She felt tight everywhere, tight as a drum, and she was grunting and moaning against the carpet like someone possessed.

Never, *ever*, had she climaxed like this. Not with a lover, not with several lovers, and not on her own. And Adelais had hardly even touched her. What would happen if it was Adelais's hand between her legs? Adelais's *mouth*?

Tate didn't know if she'd survive it. She'd only barely survived this.

Once Tate had reached adulthood at Far Hope, she'd been initiated into its secret life, and she'd gradually learned how to serve as the sisters here served, how to officiate the ceremonies that were the true heart of Far Hope. And so in the name of delivering sacred pleasure to the abbey's pilgrims, she knew much and had done much. Had thought she understood her own desire as thoroughly as a swordmaster knew their own sword.

But this was like drawing her sword to find it had turned into a glowing brand instead; this was her desire wrought into a shape she'd never before seen. And the force of it terrified her.

Tate rolled over onto her side, feeling as wrung out as a rag, her hand still between her legs and her sides heaving.

When she finally managed the strength to look at Adelais, the warrior was sitting with her legs spread, her flushed sex barely visible under the shadow of her tunic. She was licking her own fingers now, and Tate wondered if she'd brought herself to a second culmination watching Tate fuck herself.

The thought sent a shudder through her, followed by a fresh wave of heat.

"You are a surprising thing, little mouse," Adelais said, nudging at Tate's limp leg with her foot. She finished cleaning her hand and looked at Tate for a long minute. "What were you thinking about? When you came?"

That Tate could be embarrassed after what she'd just done was ludicrous, but she was. Her face burned and she rolled it into the carpet, too exhausted and sex-drunk to summon up her usual reserve, her mask of dispassion.

Adelais pounced. There was no other word for it—one moment she was on the stool, and the next she was over Tate, her body covering hers and her mouth near Tate's ear. "Oh, you have my attention now, abbess. Tell me. Were you thinking of someone licking your cunt? Maybe several some-ones? Were you half hoping I'd drag you back to Normandy and lock you in my castle?" It sounded like she meant the last part as a jest, but Tate still pressed her face into the carpet even farther. The humiliation and still-simmering lust were mingling together now, impossible to decant separately. They felt almost exactly the same.

The Wolf had gone motionless on top of her, and then lifted herself up enough to roll Tate onto her back. "Dragged off and kept," she said. "I wouldn't have guessed. What else?"

Tate closed her eyes. It was unbearable that someone else

was seeing this about her in the same moment she was learning it about herself.

"Forced, maybe?" the Wolf said softly, leaning close and biting Tate's jaw. "Taken on the road or perhaps in your own bed. Pinned and used. Someone's plaything to fuck rough and mean until they're done with you."

Tate couldn't make herself confirm it, but then Adelais bit her jaw even harder. Tate found herself whispering, "Yes. Yes."

Adelais sat up abruptly, wearing a grin that was half glee, half anticipation. All danger.

"Get dressed, my wicked nun. Go back to your sisters. I enjoyed tonight, and I enjoyed it far too much to consider clemency now. You should be here tomorrow night at dusk if you want another day of peace."

Shame washed through Tate, but it knotted with something dark and urgent too, making her all tight and needy and miserable as she stood and found her clothes.

"I keep my word," Tate said after she'd dressed. Adelais was back lounging at her stool, her linen braies on but her chausses still scattered on the floor. "I'll be back tomorrow."

"I keep my word too," Adelais said, but it sounded more like a warning than a promise. "Good night, abbess."

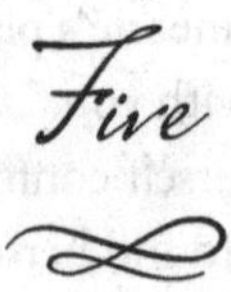

Five

THE WOLF

IF SHE DIDN'T FUCK AGAIN, Adelais was going to tear this entire valley down with her bare hands. After a few hours' restless sleep, she gave up trying, rolled her blanket between her legs, and ground against it until she came, hoping that would take the edge off until she could have the abbess again.

Adelais couldn't remember the last time she'd been so obsessed with a person, when all her thoughts had bent toward a single someone like smoke following the wind. Certainly not her husband. Handsome and charming though he was, Gérald had never piqued Adelais's curiosity. She'd had a full sense of him from the moment they met at their betrothal negotiations, and never in the four years of their marriage did he reveal anything more than what she saw that first afternoon: a swaggering libertine who was better with his cock than with a sword, who fought like a rag doll and skirted responsibility like a teenage boy.

No. Not her husband. Not even Maud, the companion

who shared her bed for a few years after Gérald's death in battle. Maud, too, had been a fine lover, energetic and flexible, and intelligent enough not to be tiresome, but she was like every other person Adelais had met in her life. Tame, predictable. A leaf fluttering when the wind blew, with all their variegations and veins visible for anyone who had eyes to see.

But Tate...

Tate was no leaf, no easily deciphered puzzle or transparent piece of glass. Her cleverness in sneaking into the camp, her pluck in daring to ask for Adelais, was nothing Adelais would have expected from the small, reserved woman once she'd met her. In fact, nothing that Tate had done at any point last night was something Adelais could have predicted, could have extrapolated from whom the nun seemed to be.

For the first time in her life, Adelais couldn't read someone, couldn't predict their words and actions. For the first time, someone was a challenge.

Or something better—a *secret*.

Adelais rolled onto her back and replayed the memories in her mind. Tate's hair in Adelais's hand; Tate's hot mouth, slick and clever. That delicious little confession as she lay panting on the carpet.

Forced, maybe?

Yes. Yes.

As much as Adelais loved secrets, she often found her interest vanishing the moment she overturned whatever stone was hiding the truth. Once she'd answered the question, there was no game left to play, no more light filling up her mind, and so she moved on to the next thing.

But that hadn't happened with Tate last night. Adelais had managed to rip the abbess's control into a pile of shreds and see the little Venus trembling underneath, full of carnal torment. She'd lifted Tate's mask, and then she'd been equally fascinated with what she found underneath. And now she had even more questions, was itching to know more and to *have* more; she wanted the little nun in front of her so she could quiz her on where she'd learned to be brave, where she'd learned to fuck, if anyone else knew what she'd confessed to Adelais last night with her own hand still pressed between her legs.

Forced, maybe?

Yes. Yes.

Agitated with want—with every hour between now and dusk seeming to Adelais a vast, horrible epoch—she finally readied herself and strode out of the tent to check on her men. They were mostly good soldiers, handpicked from Gérald's lands in Normandy and hardened by battles both in France and England, although there were a few newer men with whom she wasn't impressed, like the guards who were caught unawares by a nun last night. A *nun*.

Even though she planned on excoriating them for it later, it did make her smile now to think of. Tate slipped into their camp like a ghost, sly-footed and quiet like a holy little assassin. Sisters in Normandy were wellborn women who spent their days with needlework and prayer; perhaps they were a different breed here in England. Another thing she wanted to ask Tate.

No, not ask. She wanted more than an answer—she wanted to *know*. Intimately. She wanted to feel the girl's history as if it were her own, to be able to say with confidence what every hour of Tate's day looked like, where her favorite spot in the abbey was, where she roamed in the hills when she was free and what thoughts she thought when she stared at the sun sliding down the cloud-streaked sky. Adelais wanted to find every chemise, habit, and veil Tate had ever worn and touch them to her own skin to see how they felt, whether they were rough or soft, itchy or cool.

Whether they still smelled like Tate—like wet stone and incense.

Adelais reached the edge of camp and found Ernouf, her second-in-command, staring at the road leading the opposite direction of the abbey. It was the road they'd taken to come here, a narrow lane that wound alongside an equally narrow river.

"Has the duke sent any summons?" Adelais asked. She was given rein to come out this far, since it served William's purposes to have her terrorizing the countryside, but if he needed her at Exeter, she would be obliged to come.

"He's the king now," Ernouf reminded her, but he didn't take his eyes off the road. No, not off the *road*—off the standing stone that kept watch over this end of the valley. The company had passed by it on their way in last night, and many of the men had crossed themselves as they rode under its moon-cast shadow, as if terrified some pagan priest was going to pop out from behind it and curse them all to burn in a wicker giant.

"He's still the duke where we're from," Adelais said, "and more importantly, he's not here to hear what we call him."

Ernouf sighed but answered her first question. "No, he hasn't sent for us. But the men are wondering how long we'll stay. The valley makes them uneasy."

"Because it's difficult to defend?" Adelais shook her head. "I do not think we'll have any trouble from the locals. Anyone who can fight is in Exeter now, waiting for Harold's sons to conjure an army."

"They're not afraid of a fight, Adelais," he replied, "but of this place. It's an unholy place, they are sure of it."

Adelais laughed. "Because of a single standing stone? Have they not been to Brittany? You can't walk for tripping over a cairn or a stone table there. They're no more haunted than the aqueducts and theaters the Romans left behind."

"It's the dead and past in Brittany," Ernouf said slowly. "But it's not the past here, and it's certainly not dead. Can't you feel it? There's something different about this valley."

"There's nothing but an *abbey* down there," Adelais said, amused that solid, serious Ernouf believed in superstitious nonsense. "Founded by Alfred of Wessex himself. I can't imagine a coven of Druids taking shelter nearby, waiting for unsuspecting foreigners to wander in so they can burn us alive while they chant at the moon. And in any event, we'll only be here two more nights before we either raid or leave. Tell the men to hang on to their balls until then."

"Do these two nights have anything to do with the abbess who visited your tent?"

Adelais grinned. "A general never tells her secrets."

"Hardly a secret when the whole camp can hear."

"Ernouf, is that judgment in your voice? From you, a man with a lover in London, two in Rouen, and a wife back home?"

Ernouf gave her a look. "None of them are nuns or monks or priests, Adelais."

"It was an offer *she* made," Adelais said, clapping him on the shoulder. "I'm sure God won't mind so much, if it was to keep her abbey safe."

"Will it?" he asked. "Keep her abbey safe?"

"I thought this was an unholy place, abbey included. You care about its safety now?" she asked, lifting a brow.

"I never said the *abbey* was unholy," responded Ernouf. "But perhaps if the abbess came willingly to your bed, then…"

Adelais's smile grew larger. "Then what? Then it must be a pagan abbey? This may be a strange place, but it's not that strange. And I hardly think their saintly King Edward would have made so many pilgrimages if this were secretly a shrine to Diana or Bacchus."

Ernouf shook his head. "You may be right about that, but

there's still something uncanny here. The men feel it. I think you'd feel it, too, if you let yourself."

Adelais clapped his shoulder and turned back to the camp to check on the other men. Ernouf could keep his superstitions. The only thing she felt was a gnawing need to have her little abbess naked again.

Six

TATE

JUDITH AND LEOFGIFU had the abbey well in hand, but Tate still hesitated as she climbed up the knotty path to the moors. Her duty was to the abbey and everyone in it, and now that duty called her to the Wolf's tent. But it still felt wrong to go tonight. Not because she worried that God would judge her for the deal she'd struck with the Norman warrior, not that at all.

It felt wrong because it *didn't* feel wrong. Because there was a twisting excitement in her stomach as she crested the lip of the valley and came out onto the moor. Because her cunt was already wet thinking of Adelais.

It didn't feel like penance or payment for her crimes. It didn't feel anything like what atonement should feel like. And for that...for that, she wasn't sure if God would forgive her. To begrudgingly save her abbey was one thing. But to think about their invader finding her in the dark, tearing off her clothes, marking her with a wolf's bite...

To *want* that...

This time, she was spotted almost as soon as she left the shadows clinging to the hillside. The same two guards from last night—with grim expressions that made Tate wonder if they'd been censured for their lack of awareness the night before—led Tate silently to the Wolf's tent, and they lifted the flap for her.

Adelais was inside, sitting on her cot with an apple in one hand and a dagger with an unornamented metal hilt in the other. Tate stepped through the opening, wondering if she should take off her clothes right away or drop to her knees to signal her willingness.

Adelais sliced off a paper-thin round of apple and ate it, regarding Tate with eyes made bronze by the light of the brazier. "Let's go for a walk," she said abruptly, standing.

Tate stared. "A walk? But—"

Adelais was already pushing past her, apple and dagger still in hand. "Come on, abbess."

Adelais looked unfairly beautiful in the dusk light filtering in from the open flap of the tent, her red hair hued violet by the encroaching night, freckles like spatters of blood on her face, shadows clinging to the underside of her full mouth. She was tall and lean, and she wore nothing under her tunic, so Tate could easily make out the high, firm curves of her breasts. The stiff tips of her nipples.

Maybe Adelais would make her suck them tonight.

"Very well," Tate heard herself say in a faint voice. Who was she kidding? With the fire burning in her belly and with her own nipples pebbled and eager, she would have followed Adelais anywhere. All the way to the sea if it meant touching her again.

Adelais nodded, holding the flap of the tent so that Tate could duck out, and then Adelais followed. Together they walked to the edge of the camp and to the road leading down to the rest of the valley. They passed soldiers sitting in circles around fires and chattering; they passed the horses grazing quietly near the water, and soon they were alone in the near darkness, with only the moon for company.

As the Wolf walked, she cut off pieces of apple, her knife bright in the dark, and popped the pieces in her mouth, crunching the fruit with jaunty aplomb. Twice she offered a bite to Tate, and the second time, Tate relented and murmured, *Yes, that would be nice*.

Adelais stopped and held the slice between her fingers. "Open," she said to Tate, and Tate did, parting her lips obediently.

Adelais put the apple on Tate's tongue, and then watched as Tate closed her mouth and ate. It was as thin as a communion wafer, as sweet and tart as Adelais had tasted last night. Tate swallowed.

Adelais wiped her blade on her tunic and sheathed it. She licked her fingers clean of any remaining apple juice, her eyes full of glimmers from the moon overhead as she watched Tate watching her. Her tongue was a pale pink in the moonlight as it slid against the pads of her fingers and over her knuckles.

Tate couldn't think a single thought for a moment, she was so entranced by that tongue. And then she wanted to shake herself until her teeth rattled. What was wrong with her? Why was it this one person—this *Norman, murdering person* —could make her feel like she was drowning? When even princesses and kings couldn't do that?

She needed to get back to the way she'd been yesterday before she met Adelais—determined, emotionless. *Penitential*.

Because all of this, being the abbess and a nun in the first place, was supposed to be about penance.

She wouldn't be unraveled by a horrible Norman, and she'd decided that she couldn't allow herself to enjoy what was meant to be a duty. A sacrifice.

To do so meant—

Well, she didn't know what it meant exactly, but it still felt wrong.

"We should go back to your tent," Tate said as Adelais started walking again. She had to take two strides for every one of the Wolf's. "So we can honor our, um, arrangement."

A smile flashed in the dark. "And we need a tent for that?"

Tate's whole body felt blistered by fire, even though the night air was cool. She looked away, trying to gather herself. Trying not to think about Adelais on top of her, nothing but shadows and teeth in the moonlight.

About how wrong and thrilling it would feel to be held down in the dark...

They passed the menhir—the standing stone at the foot of the road leading to the abbey—and then turned. Soon they were on the moors, wild and undulating, a rough sea of grass and gorse and stone.

Adelais came to a stop, her eyes on the heath and the patchwork of fields carved out of its grasp. "It *is* beautiful here," she murmured, seemingly more to herself than to Tate. "A naked, wicked land."

It was the last thing Tate had expected the earthy soldier to say. It was almost...poetic. "What?"

Adelais's mouth curved, though her eyes stayed on the landscape. "It's what William's pet abbot told me when I asked him if he'd ever heard of Far Hope. He told me it was wicked place in a naked, wicked land."

Tate had a guess as to which abbot that was. "Lanfranc."

Adelais's eyebrows lifted. "You know him?"

She did, unfortunately. "There are rumors William will make him the next archbishop of Canterbury, in which case, he'll want the English church to be reformed." *Again*. Far Hope had managed to squeeze past the monastic reformations of Dunstan and Aethelwold a few generations ago, mostly because it had the protection of the king. But now the king of

England was a Norman foreigner who'd never been to Far Hope and possibly didn't know of its mission and its blessings. Could it survive another overzealous reformer with continental ideas?

The Wolf laughed. A short, bright laugh that sounded far too merry to come from the mouth of a murderer. It was lovelier than any hymn Tate had ever heard. "I don't want to wound you, abbess, but if you're an example of the English church right now, perhaps a little reformation wouldn't hurt."

Tate wasn't wounded in the least. She knew how it all must seem; there was a reason Far Hope hid itself. "Far Hope stands apart," she said. "We are the only abbey I know of like this." And then she pressed her lips together. That was almost saying too much.

"Full of angel-faced nuns ready to tempt good Christians into lust?"

Tate didn't answer. There wasn't an answer she could give that wouldn't result in a hundred more questions. Questions that she wasn't supposed to answer, although she did wonder what Adelais would think of Far Hope. Maybe she'd be delighted. Maybe she'd laugh that bright, merry laugh again.

"No matter," Adelais said. "If you are the flower of the English church, then I will pray that Lanfranc never attacks the beautiful, carnal root. Although I have to warn you that my prayers aren't worth very much."

"I could help you with that," Tate offered, and Adelais's smile widened.

"A sweet offer from a wicked girl." A step closer, gold eyes nearly silver in the night. "Now tell me, abbess. When you were thinking about someone forcing you last night, what did that look like?"

The question was clear, direct. Abrupt enough that Tate could guess that Adelais had been wanting to ask it all day.

Which meant she'd been thinking about Tate's shameful admittance in the tent all day.

Humiliation ran down the inside of Tate's chest like wine down the sides of a goblet. But it was followed by a hot rush of excitement, a thrill so twisted and dark that it brought even more shame sluicing down along with it.

Was this what forbidden things felt like to everyone else? Was this what a transgression felt like? Tate came from Thornchurch—Thornchurch, where Beltane was still marked with fire and flesh, where Imbolc and Lammas and Samhain meant bacchanals with the entire village participating. When she'd been accepted as a sister to Far Hope, she'd understood its unique blessings immediately, and unlike many other sisters and most of their pilgrims, she hadn't had to unlearn shame about her body and its desires.

But Far Hope wasn't some orgy of limitless hedonism. It was a holy place, a place of God, and chief of God's laws was free will. Was *choice*. And so to fantasize about free will being taken away felt sinful beyond almost anything else. Not the chief of Tate's sins, certainly, but close.

Adelais touched Tate's cheek, and Tate wondered if Adelais could feel the flush there. "I'd tell you there's no need to be shy," Adelais murmured, "but I'm enjoying your bashfulness immensely."

"I'm not *shy*," Tate said, trying to sound firm. In control. "But I don't know how to answer your question."

"With the truth, of course," Adelais said brightly and dropped her hand. "It's not so hard. When you were thinking of someone grabbing you and taking you, what does that look like? What would you want it to feel like?"

"I—I don't know. It's too new."

Adelais seemed to like that last part, her tongue going idly to her incisor as she studied Tate. "Too new. As in, last night was the first night you thought of such things?"

There didn't seem to be any point in lying about it. "Yes."

The Wolf's eyes gleamed. "I don't know if I should be honored or ashamed to bring out such thoughts in such a quiet little mouse, but there we are. Now, back to my question. There must have been *something* you thought of. Something that's haunted your thoughts ever since."

It had haunted more than her thoughts. Her body had been thrumming all day.

She couldn't say that out loud though; she didn't dare to —and then somehow she was. She was answering Adelais, even as she knew she shouldn't. "Your hand." Her voice was quiet. "Over my mouth."

Adelais looked very much like a wolf then, eyes avid, body still. A stillness that lured prey into a false sense of safety.

"You on top of me, pushing my shift up to my hips." Now that she'd started speaking, it was hard to stop. It was almost like a confession, really, this moment, laying a sin bare and having someone absolve her. Even if Adelais's absolution was not prayer but hunger. "You going between my legs in the dark and telling me to be quiet."

Adelais remained frozen, but Tate could see her swallowing. Could see the pulse pounding at the collar of her tunic.

"If this had been two hundred years ago..." Tate stopped; she couldn't finish. Even after admitting the rest, it felt impossible to speak aloud.

But she didn't have to. With her eerie prescience, Adelais already seemed to know. "You'd like to be carried off like a spoil? Carted off to my home, made into a concubine?"

"It's not—it's only—" Tate still couldn't find the words, but panic was what was choking her now. It felt so *awful* to hear, to have it phrased so bluntly, when in her head it was not the bleak truth of what had happened to her religious sisters centuries ago, but something else. A smear of urgent images and feelings, a blur of quickened breaths and wet flesh that ended with everyone replete and pleased.

But again, Adelais seemed to sense Tate's turmoil. "Shh, abbess, don't fret. I know you don't really want that. What you want is to play a game."

A game. Tate hadn't thought of it like that. "It doesn't feel like a game in my mind," she said slowly.

"Some of the best games don't," said Adelais. "But that doesn't change what they are. Playing, but with a beginning and an end. Playing with rules. For instance"--she came closer, her fingers sliding up Tate's neck to cup her jaw over her wimple--"a rule that you could stop the game whenever you wanted."

"And how would I do that?" Tate whispered. Adelais's hand was so warm through the thin linen, so illogically warm in the cool night.

"You'll simply say *stop*," Adelais said. She said it in her Norman tongue, *arestes*, and then said it again in Tate's English, as if to make it absolutely clear. "Stoppast."

"And you would stop? Easy as that?"

Adelais nodded. "I fight fair, and I play fair. I swear both those things are true."

Tate gave her a look. "You do *not* fight fair. I'm servicing you for three nights to keep you from pillaging my abbey."

Adelais grinned. "We struck a *bargain*. What is not fair about that? Come, abbess, what do you say? Don't you want to see what it feels like? To have what you thought about last night?"

Tate shifted on her feet. She did want it, more than she could express, because once her brain had conjured the image of Adelais's hand over her mouth, she hadn't been able to think of anything else. Like wine that could not be undrunk, the idea could not be unthought. The fantasy, however new, however blurry, could not be buried, and since last night,

Tate's mind had been full of every way it could happen. Every way Adelais could do those awful, forbidden things to her.

"Maybe," Tate said, closing her eyes. The Wolf's hand on her jaw was warm, firm. She could feel the strength in it, the threat. She'd have to pray on her knees for years for it, but the danger inherent in that touch made her something both more and less than herself—a mixture of boldness, fear, shame, and hunger. She felt like she didn't know herself.

And for the first time in ten years, she wanted to know herself.

"Yes," Tate whispered. "Not *maybe*. The answer is yes."

Adelais touched her forehead to Tate's. She was tall enough and Tate was short enough that Tate had to tilt her face all the way up, and when Adelais's mouth brushed over hers, she could almost imagine it was the night itself kissing her with its apple-sweet lips.

"What do you want, little mouse?" Adelais murmured against Tate's mouth. *Petite suriz.* "Tell me what game you would play. Tell me what it could look like out here, in the dark."

Tate could barely breathe, the words were that dangerous sliding around on her tongue. "You could be a stranger on the road," she managed to say as she opened her eyes. "I could be returning to the abbey after running an errand."

Adelais nipped at Tate's lip. "I could offer to walk you back."

"And then you could..."

Tate didn't finish. It was speaking sin aloud. Laughing at God's gift of free will to want such a thing.

Adelais lifted her face from Tate's and looked down at her. "You have to tell me the game you want to play so I can make sure we play the same one. Do I demand payment for my protection? Or do I not even bother with a little nicety like asking?"

Tate flushed. It was a cruel gift of the Wolf's, that she could see these stains in Tate's mind. And yet once the stains were out in the open, they were no longer stains at all, but possibilities. *Games.* "You wouldn't bother," Tate said quietly. "You'd take what you wanted."

"Mm. I would. Do you want to run? Would that be exciting for you?"

"I think—" Tate had to order her thoughts. She couldn't believe they were just *talking* about this, about the things that were supposed to stay in the deepest reaches of the night. "I think I'd like to try."

"Do you like pain?" Adelais asked the question like she was asking Tate if she wanted her wine watered or not—something that casual, that easy to do or not do. Gratitude twisted through Tate for that casualness. She sometimes suffered devotionally, like many monastics did, by striking her back with a knotted rope as she prayed, or wearing a leather cord beneath her knee, but suffering to creep closer to God was very different from...this.

"Some pain," decided Tate after a moment. "Enough for it to feel real. Teeth, pulling my hair, wrestling. Some light bruises, maybe."

"Good girl. Say *stop* if it gets to be too much." Another quick grin, and then Adelais bounced on the balls of her feet. It was so youthful, almost boyish of her, like Tate had just agreed to spar outside before dinner. Like Tate had just agreed to sneak into the neighbor's orchard to steal apples. Like what they were about to do was harmlessly naughty.

"And you *will* stop if I ask?" Tate checked.

Adelais gave her a sweeping, courtly bow. "Upon my honor, madam."

"I can't believe I'm trusting someone with a band of soldiers camped outside my abbey."

Adelais lifted a shoulder. Under the tunic, Tate could see

the firm muscles of her body. "I have kept my word about our arrangement, have I not? And you can share anything you like with me, because I won't tell a soul. Think of me as a confessor of sorts." Another quick grin. And then she took Tate's shoulders and spun her around so that she was facing the road to the abbey. They were at least a mile or two away from the camp, and all around them was the great emptiness of the moors and hills. "Go. And your stranger shall catch up with you."

Tate sucked in a breath. She wanted that. She wanted it so much that nothing else mattered. Not even that it was the Wolf, of all people, giving it to her.

And strangely, absurdly, she trusted Adelais. She shouldn't —she knew she shouldn't trust a murderer, a Norman, someone who wanted to crash through the gates of her abbey and violate its halls. But she also didn't get the sense that Adelais was interested in hurting any of her sisters in the process, and maybe that mattered.

I fight fair.

In a war, that mattered a lot.

And more than anything else, Adelais was right: she hadn't gone back on her word. Tate respected that, found comfort in it. She didn't mind a villain so long as they were honest about their own villainy. It was how she felt about herself, after all.

She started walking, forcing herself to keep her eyes ahead, her steps regular and even. She wanted to dawdle and she wanted to run. The more space she put between her and the Wolf, the more the anticipation prickled her flesh, and she didn't know how to alleviate it. Let herself be caught quicker? Give in to her fear and bolt?

No. No. That wasn't the game...or at least not how the game was supposed to start. The game started with her innocently walking to the abbey. She didn't know she was being hunted yet.

After another few minutes, she heard them. Footsteps from behind her. Lighter than any solider should walk, but they weren't careful or measured. These were the footsteps of someone confident, someone cocky. Someone who felt like they had all the time in the world to do what they wanted.

Tate's heart was beating faster than hoofbeats on the road when she turned to see Adelais's shadow coming closer. Adelais wore only a tunic, hose, and boots, with her dagger belted at her waist, and Tate could see the tight power in those legs as she strode closer. She could see the small nip of her waist and the slight flare of her hips.

"Hold," Adelais said. Her voice wasn't higher or deeper than it normally was, but something about it sounded different to Tate. Maybe that was her own overactive imagination, already panting after what would come next. "Are you going to the abbey?"

Tate's fingers rubbed nervously against her palm. "Yes."

"Alone? At night?" Adelais stopped and cast a look around. It was a look a helpful stranger might give, a look that said, *See how dangerous it is out here? I'm worried for you!*

It also made it seem like she was checking to make sure no one else was nearby.

A chill ran up Tate's spine and then down again, meeting the heat blooming between her legs.

"I know the way," Tate managed to say.

"Any way is dangerous if the wrong people are on the road," Adelais said, all concern. "Let me walk you there. I want to make sure you're safe."

"I promise I'm safe," Tate said, and Adelais merely shook her head.

"Don't make promises you can't keep."

Nodding her acquiescence, Tate started walking again, keeping to the side of the road so that there would be room for Adelais to walk next to her. The moonlight shone on them and on this next stretch of road before it dipped into a thickly wooded valley, a place of utter darkness despite the moon.

There. It would happen there.

But when Tate looked over at Adelais, she was still walking with the jaunty steps of a traveler on an easy journey. Not at all like she was planning what their game called for. Adelais was *good* at this, Tate realized. Good at playing the part, good at pretending. But it wasn't pretending like priests did for the Easter plays, woodenly acting out a part already written for them. Adelais wore this self, this stranger-self, as easily as clothes, her entire body moving loose and carefree, her demeanor completely different from the blunt soldier of the camp.

It sent a strange sort of pang through Tate to see. It was beautiful, and it also filled Tate's chest full of ...tenderness? How many selves did Adelais have inside her? How many other people were privileged enough to see them?

"Where are you traveling to?" Tate asked, unable to keep her eyes from the Wolf for long. Adelais's hair was as it was last night—the sides braided back and away from her face, the rest loose in long, scarlet waves—and her face was like something from a myth. A Valkyrie, an Amazon. Lovely and deadly to behold.

"Oh, here and there," Adelais said lightly as her stranger-self. "Wherever my will to wander takes me."

"This is a lonely place for wandering."

"I find the loneliest places have the most arresting diversions."

That last reply was said just as lightly, just as casually, but a darkness threaded through the words. Tate's heart was beating so fast that she was sure Adelais could hear it. She couldn't stop her eyes dropping to Adelais's hands, long-fingered and strong. She suddenly couldn't remember anything ever being more erotic than those hands, than the way they looked in the dark right now. Deceptively innocent.

The Wolf's hands and a stranger's hands at the same time.

"I don't think there will be much to divert you here," Tate said, not as good at playing her part as Adelais was at hers but liking the way it felt anyway. She wasn't an abbess forced into a job she never wanted. She wasn't the only person who could keep Far Hope alive in these cursed times. She wasn't a murderer, still trying ten years later to claw God's forgiveness to herself.

She was just a sister trying to get back home. A mouse hoping all the cats were asleep.

"Oh, I don't know," Adelais said. They were very close to the wooded section of the road now. Shadows were beginning to pool at their feet like the lapping waves of the sea. "I've already got my eye on something."

Tate held her mantle closer, reached up and adjusted her wimple. Then, quicker than she could understand it happening, Adelais's hands were on her head, one on her jaw and the other plucking at the pins in her veil and her wimple.

"What are you doing?" Tate said, trying to twist away. The hand on her jaw was too strong, however, and she couldn't move without hurting herself.

"I want to see your face," Adelais said simply. With brisk, expert movements, she had the fabric unpinned, and soon Tate's entire head was bare. "There, isn't that better? Don't you feel better?"

The minute Adelais released her jaw, Tate reached for the crumpled fabric, but Adelais held it out of Tate's reach.

"Now, now," tutted the Wolf. "I've just gone to all that trouble to see you. No sense in covering up again. Who's here to see? Your sisters? Your abbess? Surely, they've seen more. Surely they've seen you bathing, in bed at rest. They won't be shocked by the sight of your hair."

"It's not proper," Tate protested. That part wasn't just for the game; it was true. Uncovered hair meant wantonness to most people, and however much Tate knew about the secret holiness of what other people might consider wicked, wearing a veil was a hard habit to break when she was outside the abbey walls. Which was rarely.

"Do you think a lot about what's proper?"

Not in the way Adelais meant, not in the way the game meant...but did Tate find herself consumed with duty, with penance, with forgiveness?

"Yes," Tate said. "I try to do what's right. It's dark here," she added hesitantly. "We should keep walking."

"Are you afraid of what will find you in the dark?"

Nothing could be more frightening than her own memories, and it was in the dark that they visited her the most. "Yes."

Adelais clucked. "Poor thing. I'll keep you safe." Adelais's hand found Tate's, clutched it. The possession in the seemingly innocent touch sent heat flaring up Tate's arm to her throat and face. "You're cold."

"I'm fine."

"I could warm you up."

Tate tried to pull away. "I'm not cold, I promise."

"You're lying," Adelais-the-stranger said. "I don't like lies."

"I think—I think I should go on alone." Tate didn't have to fake the tremble in her voice; it was there all on its own. Partly lust, yes, but partly fear too.

The difference was that she wanted to be afraid.

"Oh, no, that won't do at all," Adelais said softly. "I can't let you go, sweet thing. We've only just gotten started."

Now. Tate knew the moment to run was now.

She turned and bolted deeper into the darkness, able to make out the shape of the road only from the occasional pool of moonlight through the thick branches above. She heard Adelais's delighted laugh as Tate forced herself to run harder, faster, pumping legs that were too short. It was like racing Heorot as children, knowing she would lose because she was pointlessly, eternally, shorter than everyone else.

Adelais seemed to know it, too, her laughter echoing off the trees as footfalls pounded on the road. She was chasing Tate now, and doing so easily, judging from the sound of her laughter. "Slow down, little nun! I won't hurt you!"

It was dark, so dark, and the flashes of moonlight made everything all the more disorienting. How would Adelais capture her? And what she would do when she did?

The footfalls were so close that Tate knew Adelais was only a few feet behind her now, close enough to—

Arms, strong enough to wage war, wrapped around her waist, and both Adelais and Tate tumbled to the ground. Adelais turned, catching them on her back as they fell, although the fall was still abrupt enough to drive the breath from Tate's chest. She tried to find it again, struggling against Adelais's hold, and then, just as she drew a sharp inhale, Adelais flipped them over so that Tate was on her back looking up and Adelais was on top of her, braced on her calloused, battle-nicked hands.

"Now, look at us," scolded Adelais. "On the ground like animals." But the scolding was belied by the wicked smile on her face—visible only as the shine on the blunt edges of her teeth in the dark. She dipped her face to Tate's and stamped a bruising kiss on Tate's mouth, and then moved to Tate's neck, where she sucked at the skin. It was hot, tickling, and then sharp when she bit at the tender skin above the collar of Tate's mantle. Tate arched underneath her, needing—needing something. More pressure, more friction.

Just...more.

Adelais seemed to know, because she slipped a muscled thigh between Tate's legs as she skated her teeth along Tate's neck, and Tate couldn't tell if she was squirming to get away or squirming to rub her herself against Adelais.

Adelais grabbed the hem of Tate's habit and shoved it past Tate's waist so that Tate was naked below. She hadn't bothered to wear hose underneath; there hadn't seemed much point when she was going to the Wolf's tent. And now she was bare to the open air of the night, naked calves, naked thighs. Naked hips and cunt.

Adelais found Tate's seam with her fingers and probed. Tate could *hear* how wet she was, and she let out a broken noise when Adelais swept those wet fingers over the pearl of her clit. "Don't fight me, sweet nun. It's easier if you don't fight."

The words were like a flame to a wick, or oil to fire. Tate couldn't breathe for the fire roiling through her, and she couldn't stop her hips from arching to the Wolf's touch. Pleasure seared up from Adelais's fingertips, all the way up into Tate's belly and chest, but Tate wanted more than this, even, more than the dark and the road and Adelais's vicious words.

She tried to roll away, bucking pointlessly under Adelais's weight, and Adelais laughed again—gleeful, vicious. "We haven't even gotten to the good part yet." Her free hand went all the way up Tate's habit and squeezed her breast. Hard.

The touch was a wave of pleasure crested with a flash of pain. Adelais did it again, and again, squeezes and then hard cups, like Tate's breasts were some sort of payment that Adelais had been too long denied.

"Let me go," Tate gasped, loving how her protest made Adelais grin wider, made her touch harder and greedier.

"I'm not done with you, pretty thing," Adelais-the-stranger informed her. "Hold still."

"I won't," Tate breathed, twisting as hard as she could and managing to break Adelais's hold on her. She flung herself to the side and got up to her knees, so close to getting to her feet, and if she did make it, if she did run, maybe Adelais would be even meaner, even rougher—

She didn't make it to her feet, though, not even close. Adelais was on top of her again, this time with her chest to Tate's back, and she bore them both down to the hard dirt of the road, her thighs caging Tate's legs and her hand snaked around Tate's hip to hold her sex. To rub her. All their weight pressed Tate's cunt into Adelais's touch, adding more pressure, more force, and then Adelais reached her free hand under Tate's chest to collar her throat from underneath, which meant Tate felt held, trapped, bound. *Everywhere.* The hand wrapped around her throat, the body on top of hers. The knees fencing her legs in, the hand moving hard and merciless between her legs.

"Make my hand wet when you come." Adelais bit at her ear, her jaw, her neck, like a wolf in truth. "You can do it. I know you want to."

"No," Tate moaned. "You can't make me."

Adelais's weight shifted a small amount—her hand between Tate's legs went still. "No...or *stop*?" Her voice—still Adelais, but the blunter, slightly warmer cadence of her natural voice.

"Not stop," whispered Tate. "Just *no* like...like I want not to want it."

Adelais nipped at her ear again, but gently this time. An acknowledgement. And there was another pang in Tate's chest, something she only felt when she thought of her childhood home or stared out at the moors on a sweet summer's day.

I play fair.

Adelais was playing fair. Even when the game was this.

Her hand moved once again between Tate's legs, rubbing her stiff pearl with hard caresses, making Tate's toes curl in her boots. The warm weight of her, the hand on her throat. The rough fucking with her habit shoved up to her waist...

"You'll be my whore, won't you?" the stranger whispered in her ear. "I've been looking for one to play with for so long."

"I—" Whatever she was going to say turned into a moan. The climax was clawing at the base of her spine now, clawing all the way down her thighs. It felt better than sin and better than forgiveness; it felt like the knotted cord on her back and the whisper of God's love at the same time.

"I'm going to keep you," the stranger swore. The stranger was unstoppable, selfish, living hellfire. Tate's entire body from her chest to her knees was rigid with the trammeled orgasm, and she was almost terrified of it, terrified of how it would wreck her if it was left to charge free. But Adelais gave her no choice. A monster in the dark, with even more monstrous words. "I'm going to keep you forever and fuck you whenever I want, and your God can come to England and fight me for you himself, because I'm not giving you up."

Tate did as Adelais asked and soaked her hand as she came, screaming, bucking, wild. The orgasm almost *hurt*, clenches and contractions that took work to live through, like her entire body had become a vessel for this monster's will, like she was being possessed by Adelais from the cunt up.

Adelais didn't let up a single bit—not the grip on her throat, not the cruel stroking of her hand, not her weight pinning Tate to the cold ground. And Tate thought she could love Adelais for it, for giving her this thing that was a sword of shame and a cup of relief all at once. Like a creature out of a myth, Tate had to be torn open and reborn, and this was her rebirth, right here in the cold, dark night. With a Norman on top of her, with her country broken, with the never-ending wheel of hunger, sickness, and violence creaking over her life.

But *this*—this was hers. This was hers to have right now: the sharp, clean gasps of air into her lungs, the urgent shudders of her body, the earth beneath her face, and the branches of trees older than Wessex itself waving around her.

Yes, Tate could love Adelais for giving this to her. For giving it so easily and without judgment.

And that was something far more frightening than any footsteps in the dark.

Seven

THE WOLF

ADELAIS DIDN'T WORRY OVERMUCH about her sins, but as she pulled her hand from Tate's body, the weight of her own gluttony nearly flattened her. She wanted to make the naughty little abbess come again; she wanted to flip Tate over, get rid of her own hose, and straddle the nun's wicked mouth until she peaked.

Mostly she just wanted to crush the limp, dazed Tate in her arms and smell her sweet-scented hair and ask her everything she was feeling and everything she'd ever felt and everything she wanted Adelais to feel, too, because Adelais would try for her; Adelais would try to feel anything she asked.

But first Adelais needed to come, because if she didn't, she wasn't entirely sure she wouldn't end up fucking Tate into the road again, and she was certain Tate needed a chance to recover. So Adelais took care of herself like a soldier: with a blunt hand down her own hose and a few rough strokes. It didn't take long, not after what she'd just done, and with Tate still underneath her. It had taken her longer to lace up her boots that morning than it did to culminate, and Adelais could have laughed at herself, at her own wastefulness. Here she was with a warm, sated nun underneath her, and she was masturbating like an adolescent watching a milkmaid undress. Ah, well. The night was young yet, and she had other things she wanted to do.

Though her sex was still pulsing out its release, Adelais withdrew her hand and then lay down right there on the road, rolling Tate into her arms.

Tate went easily, sweetly, her head fitting onto Adelais's shoulder like it had been made to go there, her arm sliding over Adelais's waist, and a little sigh escaping her lips as Adelais rearranged Tate's habit so it covered her legs once again.

That sigh was a sound escaped from heaven, a note straight from David's harp. It eased the demons inside her like it had done for King Saul, and Adelais felt full of light and peace. If the Wolf of Normandy was allowed to feel such a thing.

And even though the ground was hard and the night was chilly now that they weren't wrestling or fucking, Adelais never wanted to move from this place. She would erect a castle right here on this very spot. She would fortify it and furnish it, and then they would never have to leave. They could live and die here, and hang the rest of the world. The world had gotten enough from the both of them—surely they were entitled to a little selfishness by now.

"Are you warm enough?" Adelais murmured.

Tate nodded, a sleepy arc of her head on Adelais's shoulder. "You keep me warm."

Why that made Adelais's eyes burn, she didn't know.

"Why are you a nun, little mouse?" Adelais said, her voice soft. It wasn't a true question, not really. More of a lament.

But Tate answered anyway.

"I killed a man," said the abbess quietly after a minute. "When I was fifteen."

Adelais didn't want to do anything to divert this unexpected openness; she couldn't bear the idea of getting behind the veil of Tate's innermost self only for it to draw closed again. But she did stroke the nun's soft hair, hair as dark as a lake at midnight. "I've killed many, many men," said Adelais. "Does that make you feel better?"

"It shouldn't," Tate said after a minute. "But it does. A little."

"Why did you kill this person? Did you do it to protect yourself? Your home?" Adelais pictured a bandit, a raider, some disgruntled Dane after Edward succeeded the Danish Harthacnut to the throne.

Even though it happened years ago, a storm of heat coiled in her chest at the thought of someone trying to hurt Tate. It made her want to find this person's grave just so she could kill them all over again.

"Yes, it was to protect myself, and someone else too. But my home?" Tate gave a bitter laugh. "I'm not sure anyone in my village would have ever forgiven me if they'd learned the truth. I certainly can't forgive myself."

Adelais didn't respond to this other than to hold Tate tighter against herself, like if she held her close enough, she could soothe away the years-too-late fear she felt for Tate's safety.

"He was my brother," Tate said finally. Each word came out with an exhale, like speaking them required intention, force of will. "So you see the problem now. You have killed lots of men, but this wasn't a battle and he wasn't holding a sword. My own flesh and blood, and I killed him like a coward."

"When you were fifteen," Adelais stated. "Young people don't kill unless they're told to kill or unless they're terrified.

Which was it, little mouse? Did someone tell you to do it? Or were you so scared that you didn't see any other way?"

Tate drew in a breath, and Adelais could hear the shaking in it.

The darkness, though getting colder and colder the longer they laid still, was like a blanket around them, a shroud of quiet, familiar safety. "He used to hit us," she said after a long minute. "When he was in a temper. My parents died when I was ten, and Cafnoth was the oldest, so he inherited Thornchurch. Heorot was the middle child, and maybe Cafnoth thought he needed disciplining, I don't know, but he was hardest on him. He only struck me a few times. But Heorot..." Tate paused, and Adelais wondered what she was seeing in her mind now, what she was reliving. "The day it happened, Cafnoth learned that the woman he'd wanted to marry had fallen in love with Heorot instead, and Cafnoth was...so angry. Beyond rage. He stormed into the house and grabbed Heorot and—"

Tate sucked in a breath, a short one, like her body had forgotten it was here and not there during that day. "They fell to the ground and he was trying to bash Heorot's head against the floor, and there was blood everywhere, and I grabbed a poker from the fire and I hit him. As hard as I could."

Another breath. Sharp, quick.

"You saved your brother," said Adelais. She knew she didn't always think like other people did, especially when it came to what was right and what was wrong, but she could not see the crime in this. Saint Aidan himself would have done the same in Tate's shoes.

"I could have hit Cafnoth on the back or on the arm or *anywhere* but the head," said the abbess bitterly. "I could have pulled him off, maybe, or tried to get between them. Or I could have hit Cafnoth hoping only to incapacitate him. But I didn't, Adelais. When I lifted that poker, I was *hoping* I'd kill him. I was *hoping* he'd die. I'd been so scared and so angry for so long, and not just for myself, but for Heorot too, and I wanted it all to stop. Just. Stop. And so that's what I can't forgive myself for. Not what I did, but that I *meant* what I did. That my mind was filled with as much evil as Cafnoth's."

She stopped suddenly, as if she'd run out of air, out of words altogether. Adelais understood; she'd seen her share of soldiers after their first battles, mixed up and miserable. And there were plenty of things in her own mind that never seemed to weave themselves properly with words.

"And then what happened?" Adelais asked. "You came to Far Hope?"

Tate nodded, her hair sliding over Adelais's shoulder. "Heorot and I lied and said Cafnoth had been attacked on the road and managed to stumble home before he died. Heorot inherited Thornchurch, and I entered the abbey as a novice the day after the funeral."

"Is this why they call you Tate the Pious? You've been trying to atone?" It made sense now to Adelais—the cool reserve, the too-thin body. She'd been punishing herself for ten years for something most people wouldn't lose a single night's sleep over.

"Not only for the crime of killing my own flesh and blood, but for wanting to do it," Tate whispered. "For not...for not feeling as guilty as I should."

Adelais stroked her hair, tangled her legs closer to Tate's. They would need to go soon. She didn't want Tate to get cold. "I don't feel guilty for the people I've killed," said Adelais. "And there have been many. I don't kill children, and I only kill people with a sword or axe in their hand. But they would not be dead if my king hadn't decided he wanted the English crown."

"And you don't feel guilty for that?" Tate asked, her tone more curious than offended.

Adelais would have shrugged had Tate not been on her shoulder. "War is war, abbess. How many battles has England fought in the last fifty years? Your little island is always at war. Danes, Northmen, *each other*. It is the same on the Continent. There is always fighting, and there always will be."

"I don't think there should always be fighting," Tate said. And then she exhaled. "But how can there not be, when even I had it in me to kill someone in cold blood?"

"Hardly cold blood," Adelais said. "What did your abbess say about all this when you joined?"

Tate took a minute. "That God had a plan. That Far Hope wouldn't be able to last forever as it was, and that it needed someone willing to do what others couldn't. It needed someone who wasn't afraid of death if it meant more life."

"That is what your Christ was like, was it not? He paid death for more life."

"Isn't he *your* Christ too?"

Adelais made a noise. She'd been baptized, and, overall, she liked God a good deal—especially in the Old Testament, when he was capricious and interesting—but her father had not been particularly devout, and her grandparents had worn mjölnir pendants under their robes rather than crosses. Their family's conversion after Rollo's treaty had been a very gradual and halfhearted thing.

"And secondly," Tate went on, "Christ paid his own life. That's very different from paying someone else's."

"Someone else who would have paid Heorot's life if he had the chance," Adelais pointed out. "Besides, I'm sure your abbess was speaking metaphorically." That was something all religious types had in common—English, Norman, or even Lombard, in the case of Lanfranc.

"I suppose she was, although I don't think she felt like Far Hope's end was a metaphor." Tate sighed. "I fear our abbey's days are numbered. Without the protection of an English king…"

Adelais shifted on the ground, a slow tide of guilt seeping up from the road to the curves of her cheeks and the tip of her nose. She was glad Tate couldn't see her flushing in the dark. She wasn't accustomed to feeling guilty over anything she did, much less anything William ordered her to do. But she was a different Adelais around Tate, maybe.

Tate sat up suddenly, Adelais's arm still looped around her waist, and looked down at Adelais. The faint, faint wash of moonlight traced that enigmatic mouth, and Adelais's body tightened. Why hadn't she taken advantage of that mouth earlier? She couldn't remember now.

"Does it truly not bother you?" Tate asked, the words filled with intensity and vulnerability both. "Being the Wolf? Having killed people?"

The guilt was joined by something else now, a kind of low-simmering panic. She didn't want to say the wrong thing and have this little nun run away from her. She didn't want Tate to look at her any differently than she was just now.

But there was no point in lying, and in any event, Tate already knew the worst of her, probably thought Adelais was even worse than she really was, given the way stories grew and changed as they got told. The truth was the only thing worth telling.

"I like being the Wolf," Adelais said simply. "I like battle; I like war. I like those frostbitten mornings when the only thing keeping me warm is the anticipation. I like someone testing my sword, my axe, and making me work for a victory." She paused, and then added, so there could be no mistake, no painting her as some reluctant warrior who'd learned to love their trade, "I wasn't born otherwise. It is when I feel the most alive."

Tate stared down at Adelais. Her eyes were nothing but shine in the shadows. "It does not haunt you? Killing people?"

"No, little mouse," Adelais said softly. "And if I had done what you had done, I would have felt proud of myself for saving my brother. I would have been relieved that Cafnoth couldn't hurt anyone else."

"But you only know kills in battle. Those are different from what I did to Cafnoth. The pope even blessed William's war—"

Adelais rolled her eyes. "A pope's blessing doesn't make a thing *right*, and that's something even a nun should know. No, I face what I've done on its own terms. I have killed, and many of the people I killed were not on a battlefield, but on the edges of some village as they tried to keep us from collecting taxes or supplies. Yes, I fight fair, but was it fair in the first place that I was there? I don't know. William and the pope think so. The people who dug the graves likely don't."

"You're very honest with yourself."

"I have to be," Adelais said. "Because the world is not honest with me."

"Because people tell stories like you're a monster?"

Adelais tucked an arm behind her head, still looking at the shadow-draped woman in front of her. She could look at Tate forever, she decided. For the rest of her life, and then she'd ask to be buried next to Tate after she died, propped on her side so she could keep looking even after she couldn't see anything at all anymore.

"I like the stories," Adelais said. "It's the things I *do* that create the Wolf, not who I was married to, who was I born to. Not the lands I hold in my son's name. Not the way people think Adelais of the Maine should be—"

Adelais stopped. Not because she wanted to stop, but because she realized she'd never explained this to someone. She'd never had to weave her thoughts about this with words, and all the words she knew were as useless as a tangled skein of yarn in a bucket of cooling wax.

"Should be?" Tate asked. Her voice wasn't gentle, necessarily, but it was open. Open like a doorway. Open like a tabernacle at Easter.

Adelais squeezed her eyes closed. Not because it was hard to talk about this so much as it took all her concentration to explain what she'd never had to explain before. "Abroad, I am William's pet monster, and back home, I am the mother of Gérald's son. And I'm lucky to have both things. I could be shut up in a bower embroidering dresses, desperate for any visitor no matter how boring, because I never get to go anywhere. Never get to travel or fight or do anything interesting at all."

Adelais opened her eyes to see Tate watching her.

"*But* sometimes I hate that there can only be a single Adelais in one place. I am many Adelaises, and I *like* being many Adelaises. And it's not that any one version of me feels wrong or anything, it's only that there are so many ways of being me that feel *right*. But I can't choose every day who I am depending on what feels right. I have to be what other people expect." Adelais thought a minute. "I suppose that's why I choose to be the Wolf as often as I can. When you're a story, then people expect you to be different, at least. And maybe that's as close as I can get."

Tate reached out and touched her arm. "You could tell me," she said in that solemn way of hers that Adelais found so hypnotic. Like she was praying over Adelais; like she was whispering a verse from scripture that had been hidden until now. "You could tell me which Adelais you are, if you are a legend or a soldier or a mother or a stranger on the road."

Adelais reached up and touched Tate's jaw.

"If only I could tell you for longer than just tomorrow," she murmured.

Tate's eyes closed, and the breeze spilled around them, cold and restless. "I am grateful for the sake of Far Hope that you are keeping your promise," she said. "But I will miss you when you go."

The guilt was hot enough to catch the sky on fire. Adelais tried to ignore it, quash it, extinguish it with cold reason. She hadn't come here expecting this little abbess, after all; she'd come here for herself and for William.

At the end of the day, she was his wolf.

"I'll miss you too," Adelais said, and it was so much the truth that it felt like a lie to speak. She sat up and took the nun's cool hands in hers, and then stood, pulling Tate with her. "We should go before you freeze. Come on."

Eight

TATE

THE REST of the night was a blur of skin and sighs in Adelais's tent. And when Tate crept back to the abbey at dawn, sore between her legs and her heart feeling like it was too big to fit inside the mew of her ribs, Adelais went part of the way with her, walking Tate to the footpath she'd take up the hills and then around to the backside of the valley.

"Do you have to go?" Adelais asked. Her hair was all the way undone now, and she wore only a thin undershirt over her hose. In the gradually brightening gloom, Tate could see the lean shape of Adelais's body through the fabric.

"I wish I could stay," Tate said, meaning it. "With you."

"Would that be strange for you?" Adelais asked. "Staying with me?"

"Because you're not a man? Because I'm a nun?" She thought for a moment. "Or because you're a Norman?"

Adelais let out a low laugh. "All three, I suppose."

That was fair. This was hardly the usual way things happened, but then again, they were hardly the usual people.

"Things are different where I grew up," Tate explained. "At Thornchurch. There weren't any limits as to who you shared a bed or a life with, at least not in the valley. And as for being a Norman, well. No one's perfect."

Adelais grinned. But the grin came with a pinning stare. "You didn't address the part about being a nun."

"And I won't," Tate replied. "Unless you do the impossible and win your bet."

"My bet that I'll learn the secrets of this place?" Adelais smiled, her hands tucked behind her back. "Hmmm."

"Good night, Adelais. Or good morning, I suppose. I'll see you tonight."

And so Tate left the smiling soldier behind and trudged back to her abbey, her home, and her responsibility.

Her prison.

Leofgifu took one look at Tate and demanded she spend the day catching up on sleep, but Tate refused, joining her and Judith for lauds, and then helping care for the sick pilgrims. But as she prayed, carried water, and cleaned bed linens, her mind was still on the road with Adelais. Her body was still trembling with a release so powerful it unraveled everything she knew about herself, and her heart was still in her throat, remembering how Adelais's voice sounded as she'd asked, *Do you have to go?*

But mostly, there was this *thing* that followed her, that was like a halo coming from inside her, but it came from her chest and her gut as well as her head, and it was this one simple revelation.

Absolution.

Tate didn't know how Adelais had bequeathed it to her, how Adelais's blunt non-judgment had done what Mother Ardith's confidence and Edwin's gentle reassurances hadn't, but somehow, it had. Tate felt lighter, brighter, like maybe forgiveness could be hers. Like maybe it had been hers a long time ago, and God had to resort to sending a Norman invader to her door to tell her so.

A Norman invader who Tate couldn't stop thinking about, couldn't stop aching for.

Tonight, she told herself. *Tonight.* And maybe—well, the Normans were here to stay, weren't they? Adelais had mentioned a son in Normandy, but perhaps it wasn't so unreasonable that she would live in England, at least some of the time. William seemed to keep his favorite nobles close, rewarded them with stolen lands and titles. Tate had hated William for it before, but if it meant Adelais stayed in England, that she could see Adelais again after all this was over...

After their noontime prayers, Leofgifu ordered her to bed. Tate made sure the pilgrims were cared for, and then staggered to her cell, barely able to wash herself and change into a clean shift before she collapsed onto her bed and darkness took her.

Her dreams were all of Adelais.

They were very good ones.

But when she woke from her happy, wicked dreams, she woke not to late afternoon sunlight, but to complete darkness. Leofgifu must not have woken her up for their afternoon or evening prayers.

Tate had needed the sleep, but now she was going to be late to meet Adelais, and that had her tossing her blanket back to roll out of bed as quickly as she could.

Except her blanket didn't flip over her legs. It barely fluttered at all. Tate blinked as the shadows at the edge of her bed began to move, resolve into a shape, tall and large, barely outlined by the faint moonlight coming in from a small, high window. A dagger hilt gleamed at the shadow's waist.

Someone was in her cell.

Someone was in her cell watching her *sleep*.

Tate opened her mouth to scream, but a hand clapped over her mouth instead. "Shh," said a musical voice in the dark. Tate smelled grass, metal, soap. "You don't want to wake anyone up, do you?"

Tate tried to speak, but Adelais didn't loosen her hand on Tate's mouth.

"You know," Adelais said conversationally, "when you didn't show up tonight, I thought maybe you'd decided not to honor the arrangement after all. That a third Danegeld payment was one too many."

Tate reached up to pull at Adelais's wrist, but Adelais caught her hand with her free one, her eyes shining.

"No, no, abbess, I'm not angry. I came here to demand my payment, thinking I'd find you defiant, hiding yourself away from me, and instead I found my little mouse curled up asleep in her nest. I must have worn you out last night."

It wasn't that the fear was leaking out of Tate so much that it was joined by something just as hot, just as torturous, a brew of the same wicked, sizzling lust she felt last night. She should be wondering how Adelais made it inside the abbey, if any other Normans were inside the walls.

Adelais seemed to sense her questions, because she leaned close to Tate and murmured, "It's only me, abbess. Now, about that payment..."

Tate squirmed as Adelais considered her.

"Whatever shall I do with this little nun I've caught unawares?" the Wolf mused. "Hmm."

Tate moaned against her hand.

"Perhaps," Adelais said slowly, "I will do whatever I want."

She lifted her hand from Tate's mouth, but only long enough to shove the blankets off and find the edge of Tate's shift. It was a threadbare thing, since it would be a sin to waste Far Hope's wealth on something as frivolous as luxurious clothes for the sisters. Adelais seemed almost offended by it as she looked at it in the moonlight; with a displeased noise, she easily ripped a long piece from the hem, leaning down and using her teeth to tear the whole strip free.

Tate was about to protest—this was one of only two shifts she owned, and she'd planned on wearing it until it literally fell apart—but then Adelais was wrapping the linen around Tate's wrists and cinching them together. Tate was bound fast, like a captive for real, although strangely the insides of her felt *unbound* now, like the knots around her wrists had unraveled something that had been choking and pinching the insides of her without her knowing it until this very moment.

Adelais sat up to admire her handiwork. "If you need to stop, say the word," she said bluntly, warmly. *Arestes*. It sounded like a secret, sacred word when she uttered it in the dark. Tate nodded to show she understood Adelais's instructions.

"Now," Adelais went on, her voice tilting darker and colder, becoming the voice of an Adelais who crept into abbeys at night and sated her lusts on the innocent nuns she found there. "What will I do with you..."

Adelais moved so that her entire body was on the cot and then crawled down Tate's body until she knelt between Tate's legs. She pushed the now-tattered hem of Tate's shift up to her hips.

"What a pretty pussy," said the Wolf. "A shame it's locked away in a convent for no one else to enjoy, hmm?"

She ran idle fingers over the topography of Tate's cunt, toying with the wet rim of Tate's opening, with the sensitive berry of her clit.

"Please," gasped Tate. "I'll give you anything."

Firm fingers pushed into Tate, and Tate's back arched clean off the bed. "You're right about that," Adelais said, a toothy smile coming with her words. "You *will* give me anything."

It felt good to resist, to say no. To be forced to take what Adelais was giving her, because that way she didn't have to ask for it, she didn't have to weigh if she'd atoned enough to deserve it. She didn't have to wonder if it was selfish to take just one thing, one moment, for herself when the abbey needed her so desperately and always would.

Adelais slid her fingers free and then braced both hands on Tate's naked thighs. She could feel her own wetness against her skin from Adelais's touch, and it abruptly felt so raw, so carnal, that she could hardly stand it. Then came the Wolf's mouth, a hot slick of tongue, and Tate uttered a broken groan. She hadn't felt someone's mouth on her in so long, hadn't felt that symphony of soft lips, slippery tongue, blunt teeth in what felt like forever. Since before Edwin had died.

Adelais ate Tate's cunt with a sort of greed that made the dynamic perfectly clear: this was not for Tate. Tate was bound and helpless for *Adelais's* pleasure, not her own, and that alone ratcheted up Tate's pleasure even higher.

Heat, tickling and seeking, twined through Tate's core, twisting up into her chest and throat. Adelais licked and swirled like Tate was the only food she'd had in years, and then she pulled Tate's clit into her mouth and sucked.

Tate cried out, squirming, reaching down to thread fingers through Adelais's hair, and then remembered all over again that her hands were tied and she could do no such thing.

Adelais lifted her head from between Tate's legs and looked up at her with shining eyes and a shining, wet mouth. "It won't do to be so noisy, sister," the Wolf said. "I'd hate to have to flip you over and make you bite the blanket as I feel this lovely cunt for myself. Are you going to be quiet for me?"

Tate nodded quickly, sealing her lips together, although she couldn't deny that the threat wound her up too.

"I think I know the problem," Adelais said, a thread of malice weaving through her words. It made Tate shiver to hear. "You've been hiding this sweet thing away from everyone for so long, and it needs to come before you can behave. Don't worry. I can help with that."

Adelais reached down to her hip, and there was a flash of metal in the dark. Tate twisted instinctively—no matter how much she trusted Adelais, no matter how much she loved this depraved game of theirs, there was no escaping the urge to shy away from a knife.

With an annoyed sigh, Adelais splayed a hand on Tate's belly to pin her to the cot. Adelais put the blade between her own teeth and held the knife in her mouth while she unpinned her cloak and wrapped part of it around her hand. "It's for your own good, beautiful." And then she did something that Tate, abbess of Far Hope, leader of secret prayers in the star-ceilinged chamber, couldn't understand. Adelais took the knife out of her mouth and licked the smooth, unornamented hilt.

Tate blinked, wondering if the darkness was playing tricks on her, if she'd missed something in her twenty-five years of life that would have indicated that hilt-licking was a sexual act.

But then it became shockingly, exquisitely clear when Adelais took the knife and gently eased the hilt inside Tate.

Never—not even since she'd been initiated into Far Hope's rites—had Tate done such a thing, had she even *heard* of such a thing, using an object this way. Not even at Thornchurch, where she'd admittedly been too young to stay at the Beltane fires past dark, had she heard rumors or whispers of anything like this—and what happened by the fires was the most popular topic of conversation among her friends before she'd left for the abbey.

And yet it was happening, the handle of the knife was moving inside her, slow and good and intoxicating. Tate had seen the wide knob at the top of the handle when Adelais had held the knife between her teeth, but now she felt the knob inside: cool and hard against her soft places, and every slide and press of it was like a bright light moving inside her.

It was different from clever fingers or a thick penis, and it felt even more depraved for that difference. It felt wonderful. She couldn't get enough of it. She didn't ever want to.

But she also couldn't move, she didn't dare, because even with Adelais's cloak-wrapped hand over most of the blade, it felt like any movement could slice her right open. So she stayed as still as she possibly could, shivering in place as Adelais slowly worked the hilt in and out of her sex.

Adelais tilted the hilt in such a way that the knob pressed into the very front of Tate's walls, and she cried out again, unable to help it. Adelais didn't scold her this time, however, and there was a wide, wolfish smile in the dark as she did it again, fucking Tate better with the handle of a knife than anyone had ever fucked her with their body before.

Still unable to move for fear of the blade, Tate trembled in place, panting, her body not her own. Her body was Adelais's now, the Wolf's, and every rush and sear of sensation felt like it was coming from outside herself, coming from heaven above. A falling star, a burning bush, all kindling deep in her core.

"Oh, abbess, I wish you could see what I see right now," Adelais said. "You getting fucked like this. It's beautiful."

Tate was past speech. Whatever the hilt was rubbing against now was so fundamental to her existence, so frantically necessary, that she couldn't even *think* of the words she might speak. There was only surviving this onslaught of pleasure, there was only holding her body ready for this, and then Adelais finished her off.

Adelais leaned forward—hand still working the hilt inside Tate—and licked Tate's clit, thoroughly polishing its little tip with her tongue and then pulling it into her mouth with a hot suck.

Tate broke apart, a quake followed by a shattering followed by another quake, and on and on, her body contracting around the thickness in her cunt like it was the only thing she could hold onto in this world, her thighs locked and her chest heaving with short, wild breaths as her body shuddered and clenched and sent shivering release to every single part of her body.

Her lips tingled, her toes and fingertips too, and over and over again she came on Adelais's knife and against Adelais's mouth; she came like no nun should at the touch of her abbey's invader.

And yet she did.

Adelais pulled away to watch as Tate finally, finally subsided, going limp as if her spirit had left her body. Adelais slid the knife free, and even in her stupor, Tate felt how careful the movement was. She was making sure no part of the blade was at risk of cutting Tate's thighs.

"A real Viking wouldn't have been so considerate," Tate murmured, barely able to move her head to get a better look at Adelais wiping the hilt of her knife on her cloak.

Adelais laughed as she sheathed it. "Hard to say. Maybe a Viking would have known good treasure when they saw it." A peremptory hand played over Tate's sex, which was slick and swollen now. "Even very greedy people can take very good care of their treasures. At any rate, I'm not finished with you yet."

She stood and pulled off her boots and hose with rough, dangerous motions. The moonlight illuminated the high curves of her ass and firm lines of her thighs as she moved, and then she was pushing Tate's bound hands over her head.

"Snap your fingers if you want to stop," Adelais said, more cheerful than cruel now, and then she climbed onto the cot.

Nine

THE WOLF

ADELAIS HAD BEEN TOO noble last night on the road, and she knew it for sure the moment she sat on Tate's pretty face. The abbess didn't protest as Adelais started riding her mouth, and her slender hands stayed open and slack in their bonds above her head, as if she wanted to make it eminently clear to Adelais that she wasn't going to snap her fingers and call a stop to this.

Adelais was glad, because even though she would stop the moment the abbess asked, fucking her mouth felt *so good*. Adelais couldn't regret how overwhelmingly stirring it had been to fuck Tate, to work that knife hilt inside that soft, wet place until Tate came, but she did almost regret how riled up she was because she couldn't last. Only a few moments working her sex against Tate's mouth, and she peaked, culminating with a grunt and then making Tate lick every last wave of pleasure from Adelais's sex until she was satisfied.

She moved off the well-used nun and cut her bonds, and

then sat on the edge of the cot to catch her breath, feeling like she'd just fought off twenty men.

The abbess sat up behind her, preternaturally quiet. She would have made an excellent thief—or killer.

Adelais supposed when it came down to it, Tate *had* made an excellent killer. Adelais only wished it wouldn't haunt her so. The thought of Tate miserable, guilty, sad—it tormented Adelais almost as much as the idea of Tate being in actual danger. Looking over at the abbess's bare feet next to hers—small, delicate, fastidiously clean—Adelais abruptly knew she would do anything to make sure Tate never felt like that again.

What that meant, she didn't know yet. And what that meant for the second reason she'd come to Far Hope...she also didn't know.

"You found a way into the abbey," Tate said. Her voice was quiet. Adelais knew from her earlier scouting of the dormitory that there were only two other nuns here, and that one of them was currently with the sick visitors. The other was at the far end of the structure and had been snoring loudly enough to wake all the sheep in Devonshire when Adelais found her.

"Last night, I followed you," responded Adelais. "I didn't like the idea of you walking alone after the game we played."

Tate's mouth moved, and Adelais couldn't tell if she was holding back a smile or a frown. "I am glad you came into my room tonight," the abbess said. "It would be a gift from God if I could spend every night in bed with you. But you shouldn't be here, Adelais. The whole point of our arrangement was for you to stay on the other side of the wall."

Adelais reached for her hose and started drawing them on. "About our arrangement," she said, not knowing how to feel. The only thing in her life she wanted more than knowing the secret of Far Hope was this nun in front of her, and she had the uneasy feeling that one would come at the price of the other. But she could not be other than what she was. She was

Adelais of the Maine, and she was at Far Hope at last. "I have something to show you. You should get dressed."

Twenty minutes later, they were padding silently through the abbey's grounds, past a stone church with stained glass windows—a rarity and a luxury this far into the wilderness—and past the abbey's stables and storehouse and kitchens. All the way to the very end of the valley, where a low stone wall and something like a lichgate guarded access to the abbey's sacred spring, which was also the source of the Hope River.

But Adelais didn't take Tate through the gate to the spring. Instead, she led Tate to the sheer face of the hill beyond. A curtain of rock and moss and stubborn gorse, and, like a curtain, it had drapes and bends and folds. And in one of those corrugations was an opening.

Tate stopped as they approached, which did not surprise Adelais. In the dark, with her homespun habit and white wimple and veil, she seemed bled entirely of color, much like this lonely landscape under the cold light of the moon.

"How did you know this was here?" asked Tate. That mask of cool composure was back, as impenetrable as the rock walls around them, and Adelais hated it as much as she respected it. Tate was protecting herself and her home, and that composure was her defense, her bulwark, and her fortress walls.

Alas, walls had never stopped Adelais.

"When I followed you last night, I stopped at the top there," Adelais said, indicating the place where the path spilled over the lip of the hills and down into the valley. It was a good path, cleverly hidden, because if she had not seen someone else take it, she would have guessed these hills to be impassable. "But tonight, when I crept down, I saw a glimmer of light coming from a cleft in the rock. I followed it here."

Tate's breathing was so even, so controlled that Adelais knew she must be deeply afraid. "Did you go inside?"

There was no point in lying. "Yes. And I want to go inside again, with you." Because what Adelais had found seemed to have very little to do with heavy psalters and dry, old prayers.

Tate closed her eyes. There was the faintest twitch around her mouth; Adelais realized she was praying. That shamed her a little.

"Yes," Tate said finally, opening her eyes. Her voice was full of resignation, which also shamed Adelais and then irritated her. She was not accustomed to shame, and she didn't like the way it felt. "Yes, I will go inside with you."

The cleft in the rock was illuminated again tonight, but very faintly. But as they stepped through the cleft and down the man-made stone steps into the earth, it gradually grew brighter and brighter until they were in a chamber lit by three braziers.

"It is your job to keep these lit?" asked Adelais, knowing that it could not be an easy job.

Tate stopped beside Adelais. In the red-yellow glow, she was a luminous thing. What would this elfin creature have become had she not been haunted by her sins? Because beauty was commonplace, everywhere; Adelais had known this since she was a child and was fawned over for her loveliness. People had talked as if she'd end up marrying a count or a duke with looks like hers, but in the end, her oft-praised beauty had only been worth a castellan. There were too many other lovely girls, and with more land and larger dowries. And fewer murderous instincts.

But whatever Tate had, it was past what beauty was, what it could do. It consumed Adelais's thoughts; it made her think stupid, foolish things. It would have captivated princes, kings. And here Tate was, the keeper of an odd little abbey in the middle of nowhere.

"Yes, although I don't know how much longer," answered Tate. "It was expensive and time-consuming enough before the invasion. But now it is nearly impossible to get the wood from farther down the valley. There's been too much sickness, too much war. So many of the people we relied on are dead. I think in the next month, I will have to decide to keep the fires lit only during Michaelmas."

"That seems...specific."

Adelais knew Tate well enough by now to catch the faintest hint of a smile. "Our abbey is dedicated to St. Michael."

"Interesting." Adelais looked around the stone chamber again. It was as large as a church, and with the three braziers burning at different points in the space, it didn't feel dark. In fact, the entire quartz-studded ceiling glittered like a sea of stars, bright and twinkling. There were piles of blankets and furs, cruets of oil, low platforms heaped high with cushions. There was a stool in the corner, as if for a harpist; there were drums, lamps, gleaming goblets stacked neatly and draped with linen. It could have been a scene from King David's court after he got his army of wives and concubines. "You know," Adelais said, the heretical thought too fascinating to let slide by, "most holy places named after St. Michael used to be sites of heathen worship. Pagan places."

Tate dipped her head in a nod, her voice betraying nothing. "That is true."

Adelais looked back at Tate. "When was your abbey founded?"

"Almost two hundred years ago, by King Alfred himself," the abbess replied promptly.

"Was there a holy place here before then?"

Another prompt answer. "Yes."

"A Christian one?"

The answer came slower this time. "No."

"So this was one of the very last places in England to convert?"

Tate took a few steps deeper into the space. The firelight gilded her skin, brought out faint notes of gold in her brown hair. "That depends on what you mean by convert," she said. She tilted her face up to the glittering, starlike ceiling. "The people in this valley were quick to welcome the priests when they came. But slower to forget the old ways."

Adelais remembered sitting on her grandfather's knee, tugging on the mjölnir pendant hanging from his robes. She'd loved the idea that they were holding on to something ancient, something *almost* lost, but not quite. She had the same feeling now. "How old were those ways?"

"In this valley?" Tate shook her head. "Even Mother Ardith didn't know, but we think long before the Romans. Perhaps the people who erected the standing stone at the entrance to the valley. Whenever it started, it never stopped. And people knew this was a place of healing, and they came far and wide."

"Because of the spring?"

"Partly," Tate said. "It's said that a drink from our holy spring will heal any ailment of the body. It's also said that a night spent under the stars of Far Hope will heal any ailment of the soul." She gestured at the ceiling so there could be no mistake as to which stars she meant.

Adelais thought of the sick pilgrims in the abbey. "Is that true? About the spring?"

"They get better here," Tate said. "But sometimes I can't be sure if that's because here they are well tended, with lots of fresh air and good food, or because there is something special in the water."

"And what about here in the star chamber? What happens to heal the ailments of the soul?"

Tate turned and looked at her, green eyes vivid in the firelight. "I think you can guess."

Adelais had lots of guesses, and they were all filthy. There were only a few good reasons to have a warm, well-lit cave stocked with soft cushions and goblets for drinking, not to mention the *oil*, and put together with Tate's fluency in sex and desire...

"If this room is for what I'm thinking, it's hard for me to imagine Rome approving."

"Rome doesn't," the abbess said, a small note of displeasure creeping into her otherwise neutral voice. "Which is rather hypocritical given the amount of sinning they get up to. But there are enough bishops—not to mention princes and dukes— who have been to Far Hope and believe in it. Until William, we could count on protection from the king himself, but now..."

She didn't have to finish. Adelais would hesitate to call William a pious man given how much blood he routinely shed, but he was a rather devoted Christian, if one measured devotion in monasteries founded and money given to the church. He would not like anything as aberrant as Far Hope, and neither would Lanfranc, his presumed pick for the next archbishop of Canterbury.

"Do all the pilgrims come here?" Adelais asked. "Into the cave?"

"No," Tate said. She adjusted a stoppered cruet of oil; it was as gleaming and clean as anything in a church. "Most come for the spring and have no idea the cave is here. Only the sisters can invite people here. Sometimes they are pilgrims, and sometimes they are known to us as guests we had before or people our guests vouch for."

"So people come here to fuck, following in the footsteps of the pagans who fucked here before them, and somehow an abbey gets built to help it along?" Adelais had to give dead

King Alfred credit: If she were going to shelter a pagan orgy site, that's exactly how she would do it.

"The abbey was built because King Alfred recognized that this was a holy place," Tate corrected. "That the way people left here after a night was a gift from God. Perhaps the pagans before the abbey didn't know it as such, but that's what it was. What it is." She paused. "He also knew that Far Hope's days were waning as a pagan site. But if it was a Christian one...an abbey...it could survive. Especially if the cave and what happens here stayed quiet. A truth known only to a chosen few."

That was also smart of old Alfred. While it was common enough to find folk beliefs not much changed or liberally mingled with Christianity out in the countryside, eventually all the old practices would die out. Or be extinguished by overeager priests. But to cloak it anew, to hide it in plain sight...

It was maybe the only way a place like Far Hope could survive.

"But surely being an abbey presents some problems. For example, your body being consecrated to God. That makes it rather difficult to lead an orgy, doesn't it?"

Tate gave Adelais a look like she knew Adelais was being deliberately reductive. "My body is God's while I'm a nun, yes. That means I use it to bless people, and to heal."

"I'm fairly certain that consecration means something is to be held apart. For God and for no one else."

Tate lifted a shoulder. "At Thornchurch, we don't make those kinds of distinctions. So when I came here, it made sense to me. Sacred things should be held apart, yes. That's what makes them special and not ordinary. But I do not think it helps anyone to pretend away their bodies. They are what we live with, know God with."

She wouldn't get any disagreement from Adelais, who

thought chastity was ridiculous. Only women were made to honor it—even in the clergy—and in any event, it seemed an unfair price to pay for someone who might want the other gifts a religious life had to offer: literacy, community, escape. God.

"But it's not just sex," Tate went on. "At Far Hope, everyone is welcome. To love how they wish and who they wish. Like how King Edward came here because it was the only place he could be with the man he loved."

"I'm living proof that someone doesn't have to go to an abbey to fuck who they want," Adelais said bluntly. She had to be careful, yes, and creative, but if she wanted a woman and that woman wanted her back, then she made it happen.

"It's not just about fucking," Tate said, voice low. "It's about being. You can be who you need to be at Far Hope. Any version of yourself. That is what blesses. That is what heals. Not the sex on its own, but the freedom of self that comes with it. The joy of seeing someone else in their freedom of self." Her eyes met Adelais's again, and they were softer than her voice. Shining with something that made Adelais's throat hurt to look at. "You would not have to choose, Adelais, for any other reason than yourself. You could be any Adelais you wanted here. Every Adelais. Far Hope would welcome them all because God loves them all."

Adelais's eyelids stung. It was such a simple thing to hear, and yet in thirty years she'd never heard it. All of her—messy, restless, never happy as only one self—could be held in one place. Not only held, but loved.

If Tate believed God could do that, that it was the point of God's people to love like that...well, then maybe Adelais could understand why Tate loved her god so much.

"You told me you were looking for a treasure here," Tate went on, looking up at the starred ceiling and then back to Adelais. "And that's it. That's the treasure. That is the gift that

King Alfred found among the people here and the gift he wanted to keep alive." An exhale. "A gift that I think is dying, despite his efforts."

Adelais understood. She understood now. The treasure wasn't something that could be picked up and carried off, that could be *owned*. Whatever happened here under the sparkling ceiling of the cave could only happen here, and after it happened, it lived on inside you. She remembered King Henri's voice when he'd talked about Far Hope, how he'd sounded haunted to her young ears.

But perhaps he hadn't been haunted at all...but more *alive*, more incarnated, for remembering his time here.

Adelais looked down at her boots. The floor was level and smooth, although undoubtedly still the floor of a cave. "I don't like the idea of Far Hope dying, now that I know what it means to you. Now that I've finally found it."

"It would be easy to blame the Normans, but maybe it was always going to happen," Tate said. She sounded tired. "It gets harder and harder to find new sisters every year, and every reformer with a shred of power has a mind to purge us from the church, either because they know what Far Hope is, or because they've heard warped versions of the truth and imagine us worshipping Bacchus and whipping each other with fresh goat hides. Even without William, this day would come." She rubbed her forehead. "I think Mother Ardith was right about Far Hope not lasting. About needing someone to do what others couldn't. Which is admit defeat."

Defeat. This same woman who strode into a Norman camp with nothing but her wimple and her courage to gird her, this same woman who played the game in the dark with Adelais, a game that asked for nothing less than raw honesty and utter trust. This same woman who'd somehow held this war-battered abbey together with her teeth when all she wanted to do was pray away her imagined crime.

That woman was talking about defeat, and Adelais couldn't stand it, couldn't bear the idea of the quiet but unbending strength inside Tate yielding now.

Because that quiet strength—*that* was piety. *That* was holiness. Not fasting or flagellation with their visible dramas, not abnegation where everyone else could see, but holding fast and holding firm when nothing else felt certain, when the way was hard and cold and stark.

Standing anchored in belief like a rock in the sea while the tides swelled and crashed around you.

Adelais had wondered that first night if Tate was truly pious, and now she had her answer: Tate was pious, and more besides. She had courage like a soldier and calmness like a king. Passion like a saint, and humility like a martyr.

That piety made Adelais's shame from earlier burn all the brighter, and it was mingled with sharp obsession, with memories of Tate arching so prettily underneath her, her thighs soft and silky as they parted for her. Memories of those green eyes, that fascinating mouth.

The nun had pricked Adelais's curiosity at first, had intrigued her, but the more Adelais saw of Tate, the more her obsession had grown, grown into something that Adelais couldn't...that she couldn't name. She couldn't even trace the far edges of that *something*, except to know that she wanted Tate in her future like she'd never wanted anything else. Not even Far Hope.

Adelais wanted to *keep* this strong, pious, fascinating nun; she wanted to be near her and with her and entangled with her for as long as she drew breath. But shimmering under that urge to have and to keep, to make sure that Tate was safe and strong and given everything she ever wanted, was the ugly, honest fear of Tate learning the truth of why Adelais was here.

Because once Tate learned that her abbey's fate had already been decided...

Adelais didn't know what to do with that fear, or even what it meant that the idea of hurting Tate, and of Tate knowing that it had been Adelais to hurt her, was the most frightening thing she'd faced since joining William's war.

But Adelais had only ever reacted one way to fear, and so she stepped forward and touched the abbess's hand.

"There's something I need to tell you," she said. "About why I came here."

Tate looked at her expectantly, and Adelais braced herself, needing more courage than she'd ever needed before.

She took a breath. "William wants me to—"

A clatter of footsteps on the stone stairs. Adelais looked up to see a sister with light bronze skin and flushed cheeks emerge into the chamber. "Someone's pounding at the gates," the nun said urgently. "Threatening to burn the walls down."

Tate gave Adelais a sharp look. "Are these your men, oh Wolf?"

At the name, the other sister slid a gaze over to Adelais. There was shock in her face, bitterness around her mouth, as she seemed to realize who Adelais was. "It's the Duke of Normandy himself," the sister said to Tate, looking away from Adelais pointedly now. "And he says he's here to see the new mistress of these lands."

"Me?" Tate asked in a faint voice.

Adelais's lungs filled with lead.

"He says," the sister said slowly, "Far Hope belongs to the Wolf now."

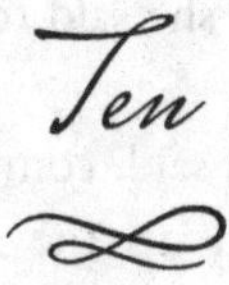

Ten

TATE

BELONGS TO THE WOLF.

The words were just sounds, just simple syllables in their tongue. Adelais apparently had a rudimentary enough grasp of English to understand what Judith was saying, because she was already trying to tell Tate something, already trying to explain.

Which was good, because Tate didn't understand.

Belongs to the Wolf?

She looked at Adelais, beautiful, strawberry-haired. Golden-eyed. Tate had thought earlier that she was like a character from a story, from a myth, but she'd forgotten.

Those myths never ended well.

"I was just about to explain everything to you," Adelais said, and her voice was still the same husky melody it always was. No trace of anything at all like an apology—although Tate could hear the intensity simmering inside the words. "I didn't want you to find out this way."

Tate tried to think, tried to shove down everything she felt and summon up the cool reserve she'd need right now in this moment. "We should go to the gates," she said numbly. "And meet the duke. The king." He was the king. He was the king and he was there to end Far Hope. To give it to Adelais.

Mother Ardith had been righter than she knew.

"Douse the braziers," she said to Judith. "He can't know about the cave."

"Tate, listen," Adelais said, coming beside her and taking her hand as they walked up the stone steps to the slow-kindling dawn outside. Tate yanked her hand back out of the Wolf's strong grip, unable to bear the affection right now. "I wouldn't have done any of this if I'd known what kind of place Far Hope was."

"So it was fine to do it to any other kind of abbey?" Tate asked. The air was cool and mild as they walked to the gates. Tate could see the torches burning beyond. "It would be fine to close a different abbey merely to add to the already endless Norman holdings stolen from English people?"

Next to her, Adelais stiffened, as if her pride were stung. Tate didn't care.

"I've earned whatever the king wants to give me," Adelais said, the words full of nettles. "You have no idea the things I've done, the blood I've given. Being given lands after courage in battle is hardly an uncommon thing."

"Yes, but they are *our* lands," Tate bit out. They were out into the courtyard now, the night gloaming into a faint dawn. All around them was the stone fingerprint of Tate's abbey on the Devonshire land, a land that had held the seeking and faithful for centuries or longer. A place where Tate had prayed, worked, buried her friends. A place a lot like where she grew up, but even better, because it wasn't haunted by her crimes. "You can't just decide to take someone's home because you want it."

"This *home* was promised to William," Adelais said irritably. "It's not our fault that Harold Godwinson decided to break his oath and steal the crown."

Beyond the gates, Tate could see a lake of fire. Hundreds of torches, dancing in the cool air. "That doesn't justify murder! That doesn't justify taking things that don't belong to you!"

"No Angle, Saxon, or Jute can be high-minded about murder *or* taking things," said Adelais. "Your kings and nobles murder people constantly, sometimes even their own kin. And don't get me started on the English and their buying and selling of captives."

Adelais was telling the truth—and was even being generous by omitting how the English had come to Britain in the first place, in a manner much like the Normans. Tate could refute none of it, but still. The *gall* of having the Wolf of Normandy say these things after Tate had just learned that same Wolf came here to steal her abbey, Tate's one home, Tate's one *reason* for hope and endurance and strength...

There was too much anger, too much shame bubbling and boiling inside her. All Tate wanted to do was scream. "Far Hope has no captives," Tate said tightly, trying so hard to hold on to her reserve and failing. "And only one kinslayer. *Me.* So what have we done to deserve being handed over to you like we're a herd of sheep and this abbey is our pen?"

"There have been no plans made about any of this," said Adelais. "I mentioned to the duke that I wanted to see the abbey, and then he told me that he wanted to give these lands to me and my son. The abbey could remain as it is, merely under my patronage instead."

"But it won't belong to itself." Tate stopped just in front of the gates, ignoring the hordes of restless soldiers on the other side. She needed to see Adelais's face when she said this, needed to see if Adelais understood this very important thing. "You've seen the deepest parts of Far Hope now. You know why this place matters. For people who need what they can't find outside our walls. For people who need help stitching their souls and their bodies together. For people who simply hunger for ecstasy and pleasure. But there's a reason this has had to stay hidden as long as it has, Adelais. It's not safe being out in the open, and it's not safe being in the hands of someone who could change their mind. Like your son, or your son's son, or his son after that."

Adelais pressed her hands to either side of Tate's face, and damn it all, those soldier's hands sent a thrill through her even now. "Tate, the abbey isn't safe *now*. You just told me that you have no guarantee that it will continue, that Mother Ardith thought it wouldn't. You are subject to the church, to the king. This abbey is in danger as it is. Let me help."

Tate stared at her. It hurt how pretty she was. "And you're going to save it? Is that how it is? You won't kick us out, but you'll be our landlord and wielder of our fate, and we should be grateful for that?"

She closed her eyes before Adelais could answer. The truth was that after the last ten minutes, she couldn't help but feel a *little* grateful that there might be an outcome less horrible than all the sisters becoming homeless. But this outcome would have a steep price. It would always be beholden to one family's whims and one family's favor with the king. Far Hope's fortunes would rise or fall along with a single other person's, and that was a dangerous position to be in. Too many abbeys, priories, monasteries, and the like had shut down for just those reasons, and if that happened to Far Hope, then everything it held on to, everything it kept in trust, would vanish.

She would fail the abbey, her home, her family. Herself.

"Give me a chance," murmured Adelais, brushing her lips over Tate's. "We could make this work. Together."

Together.

When Adelais had been keeping the truth from her this entire time.

With a sharp breath, Tate tore herself away and walked to the gate. She couldn't find the words to tell Adelais it was too late for anything like that.

* * *

The Duke of Normandy was tall, broad, and clean-shaven. He wore his hair short, had on well-made but simple clothes, and kept his large hands on the hilt of his sword and his dagger as he talked. Tate had seen enough warriors in her time to recognize one standing in front of her; she could also recognize fervor when she saw it. This was a man who believed down to his marrow—and what he believed was that he was God's chosen ruler of England. He believed that it was his destiny to strengthen the church while he was king.

But he would *not* believe the inner secrets of Far Hope were a good thing, so Tate wouldn't mention them, and she prayed Adelais wouldn't either. A prayer she wasn't sure God would answer, given how much scowling and frowning was happening in the corner of the tent where Adelais now stood with her arms crossed, listening to the duke speak.

"I trust that you will be obedient to God in this, as in all things," William was saying in Norman French. "It is my will that Adelais should have these lands, for herself and for her son. They would no longer belong to the abbey, but to her, and your abbey's income would instead come from her patronage, whatever that might look like."

"Your Majesty," Tate said, looking at his feet. It was one thing to be in a room and talk civilly with him, but looking into the eyes of the man who'd hacked and burned his way through her country scared her. Not because she was afraid for herself, but because she was afraid *of* herself. She hadn't felt anger and desperation like this since the day she picked up the poker and swung it at Cafnoth's head. "I beg you to reconsider. This abbey was founded by the great King Alfred himself. We are quiet, small, out of the way. We won't be a bother to you, and all we ask is to be left alone."

"Is that any way to speak to a king?" William said, but he only sounded irritated, not truly angry. "Come closer. I want to see your face."

Tate's very bones revolted at the order, her muscles and tendons, too, but she made herself step forward, and then step forward again until William could take her by the chin.

There was nothing sexual about his touch, nothing desirous in his gaze as he inspected her. Tate had heard he was almost obsessively devoted to his wife Matilda, that he didn't take mistresses or concubines or force himself on people. Those were all good things, except that he still forced himself on her *homeland* without mercy. So it was hard to admire him for his fidelity, however rare.

"Tate the Pious, they call you," the king murmured. "When I told Archbishop Stigand what I planned to give to my wolf, he told me that you were on the path to sainthood. A more faithful nun there never was, he said."

Tate hated that his breath smelled clean, that his face was smooth and strong, that he was reasonably handsome. Monsters should look like monsters.

She slid her gaze over to Adelais, who was scowling at the floor, red hair glowing like copper in the slowly brightening tent.

Well, some monsters looked fine just as they were.

"We are devoted, Your Majesty," Tate whispered. "We are a holy abbey, dedicated to God's will, set apart so we can bring peace to his people. Please don't tie us to the fate of the world by doing this."

William held her chin a moment longer, and then shook

his head. He released her. "I believe you. I think you are holy—maybe even holier than Lanfranc, the holiest man I know. But it is already done."

Tate had that iron poker feeling again, the tremble of rage so profound that she could swear she was shaking the earth with it. "But why *here*?" she managed to ask without screaming. "Why not anywhere else?"

"Because the West Country isn't loyal enough, because it is filled with rebels, and because I need my wolf here to keep my new subjects in line," the king said. His neutral tone hadn't changed and neither did his expression, but Tate sensed the rising conviction in him, the anger that froze and burned at the same time. Under that soldier's face was a man who truly believed these people had betrayed him by not being easy to conquer. "I need her between Exeter and the rest of Devonshire, and I also need her only a day or two's ride from the sea in case I want her in Normandy. So you see, abbess? You are not the only one whose life is not your own. Even I cannot enjoy a single Christmas in peace without some new nightmare interrupting me."

As if those things were at all the same. As if a conqueror being rebelled against by the unhappy conquered was the same as having Tate's home and her life's purpose ripped from her hands and dangled from someone else's grip for no other reason than where their abbey was built.

"No," said Tate. She met his eyes, his hateful eyes, which looked so much like the eyes of a good and proud man. "No. I cannot let you do this. This is not God's will. Archbishop Stigand—"

"Has already given me his blessing," William cut in. "I am free to move the abbey into Adelais's patronage without any fear of the church's unhappiness or God's wrath."

Stigand. That opportunistic simonist. Why was Tate surprised?

She would have to find another way. There had to be another way. She cast around for a solution, trying to think, mentally railing at God for making his church so flimsy that the word of one cowardly ballbag could determine the fate of an entire abbey.

But what could she do? They couldn't move the abbey to a new location—the valley *was* Far Hope and Far Hope was the heart of the valley. She had nothing to threaten the king with, not money or violence—or even God's displeasure, now that Stigand had already told him what he wanted to hear. Being an abbey was supposed to protect the blessings of Far Hope, shelter it from the concerns of worldly powers. But there was no recourse if the church itself acted just as selfishly as a worldly power.

"You've trapped us," Tate heard herself say. "We cannot leave our...holy spring. We cannot gainsay you or the archbishop. But Far Hope has always run itself, has always kept old ways, its own ways. I don't know what will happen to the abbey if we aren't allowed to do that, but whatever happens, it will be on your hands." She looked at Adelais, who finally, finally looked up at her.

"Your hands too, Adelais of the Maine," Tate added softly, with as much malice as she could muster.

She was gratified to see that Adelais flinched.

A glimmer of cold anger was shining in William's eyes, but he gave her a smile nonetheless. "I shall remember, Tate the Pious. God can add it to my roster of sins when I reach my judgment. Now perhaps you should return to your prayers, and within a few weeks, you will know what your new mistress will do with you and your sisters." He turned away, clearly dismissing her.

Tate didn't respond, didn't make a courtesy, even though she knew people had been exiled for less. But she wouldn't pretend that she saw him as anything other than a demon.

She pushed outside the tent into the chilly morning and sucked in the largest breath she could. And then another. And then another.

For the first time since its founding, the abbey was going to belong to someone. Yes, the king had used words like *patronage*, and other people might use words like *protection*, but there was no hiding what it really was at the end of the day: belonging.

They would belong to Adelais, and therefore to the Norman king of England, through her fealty.

"Tate," came a voice from behind her, and Tate wheeled to see Adelais outside the tent too, her cheeks flushed under her freckles from the cool air. "Are you well? Can I help?"

Tate laughed. A choked, bitter sound. "You mean like how you helped for the last three days? Lying to me about what would happen to my abbey? I showed you things I'm only supposed to show our pilgrims. I told you everything you wanted to know. And now I've betrayed my abbey to someone who'd betrayed it first. How do you think that makes me feel?"

Unhappiness creased the Wolf's face. "Don't cry," Adelais said, her eyes on Tate's face, her expression displeased as she tracked the tears beginning to streak to Tate's jaw. "I hate that you're crying. Is it truly that bad? Belonging to me? I'll be good to you, Tate. How can you doubt it?"

Truly that bad?

A broken church hierarchy, an entire conquest, and what felt like a whole world ready to pour hellfire on anyone who enjoyed pleasure on top of both those things? That bad that Tate had been ready to give this wolf her heart after only three nights alone together?

"Unless you can save the heart of Far Hope from William's grasp," Tate said, "then yes, it is that bad." She straightened, tears still dripping down her face, and looked Adelais in the eye for the last time. "And when the cave is empty and the sisters are gone and everything that made Far Hope what it was is forgotten, I hope that it was worth it to have your treasure, Adelais of the Maine. I hope that it's some comfort to think that you've found Far Hope's secrets at last, even if it was at the cost of anyone else finding them ever again."

And then she turned and went back to the abbey, tears burning at her eyes the entire way.

Eleven

THE WOLF

ADELAIS STARED at Tate's small form as she walked off, her heart like a fish on land, flapping and panicked.

She *never* felt panicked. Not in battle, not at court. This should be nothing—this should be easy. She had pleased her liege lord, and he'd rewarded her. Not only that, but he'd rewarded her with the one place on earth she'd like to own.

But here she was standing like a wounded rabbit, ready to spring away and hide, leaking blood everywhere as she went.

Hide!

Adelais of the Maine!

What had she come to?!

William came out of his tent, having to duck his tall frame under the flap.

"I want you in Exeter by tonight," he said without preamble. "I need the fear you bring to a field to end this siege. And then you may return here to make any arrangements you see fit as the new owner of Far Hope."

"Yes, my lord," Adelais said, her mind still following Tate, still hearing those pained, bitter words. *It is that bad.* "Whatever you need."

The duke studied her a moment. "It is no bad thing to go after what you want, Adelais. It's what makes you unmatched in combat."

It was indeed what made her a good warrior. But perhaps it had made her a bad lover too.

Except that wasn't the entire truth, was it? Tate liked it when Adelais *took* – she liked it all too well. But this was different. This wasn't taking something freely given. This was stealing, plain and simple, no matter which words she and William had used to make it sound more palatable.

The abbey had belonged to itself before Adelais; now it wouldn't any longer. And whatever belonged to Adelais also belonged to the king of England.

The same king who'd burned hundreds of innocent farmsteads on his way to Exeter just to show his displeasure.

"I'll keep that in mind," Adelais said, her panic solidifying into an urge to fix this, fix everything about it. "But is it possible that I could anchor Devonshire for you elsewhere? Maybe closer to the coast, like near the River Tamar—"

He held up a hand. His men behind him were readying horses; she knew she'd have to give the order for hers to be readied too. He'd expect her in Exeter soon after he got there himself, even though she had an entire camp that needed packing up first. "I want you here, Adelais, and I won't brook any further discussion on the topic."

"But the abbey—"

"We've been blessed by Stigand to do with it what we will. It's a small abbey, Adelais. We're not talking about Cluny here. If a few sisters have to find new nunneries to join, so be it."

No matter how miserable she was, Adelais had always made it a point never to waste her time on a lost angle of attack. "You are set on this?" she asked William.

He gave her a curt nod. "I am. Far Hope is already yours. And I don't care what you do with it, as long as you serve my crown above all else." He lifted a brow as a groom handed him his reins. "That includes pretty abbesses."

Adelais didn't bother to hide her irritation at that. He knew her well enough to see if she hid it anyway.

"Or," William said, mounting the horse with a strong, easy movement, "dissolve the abbey and she won't be an abbess any more. And there's part of that problem solved."

Well, he wasn't wrong—Adelais could do that. Tate would never forgive her for it though.

She might never forgive me now.

"Be at Exeter's gates as fast as you can get there," the duke said and turned his horse to face the far end of the valley, the one that led out to the road. "And forget about the nun, Adelais. Use the abbey however you see fit. Hell, make a house out of its buildings. I don't care, so long as you obey me."

She didn't even enjoy the siege.

Adelais of the Maine sat bored on her horse for four days while William's men flung arrows, dug tunnels, and died in ridiculous numbers from rebel English archers burrowed behind the walls. At one point, William blinded a hostage in full view of the city walls. At another, an Exeter guard pulled down his pants and farted at them.

War, blood, farting—it should have been paradise. She should have been in the fray, soaking it up, finding even more misadventures to plunge into, but she just...couldn't. None of it seemed worthwhile. None of it seemed interesting.

Tate was the only worthwhile and interesting thing in the entire world, and all Adelais wanted to do was spend the next sixty years watching her dress and eat and sing and walk and be, and instead she had to be here at this stupid siege, which wasn't even any fun, waiting for the dead king's mother to realize her grandsons were never coming back with the long-promised mercenaries from Ireland.

On the fifth night, Adelais finally realized the truth.

Earlier that day, she'd sat behind William as emissaries from Exeter came out with the city's surrender. "Well, my wolf?" He'd turned and asked Adelais in Norman. "Shall I be merciful and accept their surrender?"

Adelais had only been listening with half an ear; if she'd been bored by the siege this week, then she was certainly going to be bored by surrender negotiations, which didn't have any blood *or* aggressive farting, but she had heard one word repeatedly.

Fair.

The people of Exeter hadn't rebelled because they were particularly in love with Gytha Thorkelsdóttir or because they truly cared about seeing one of her grandsons on the throne. Instead, they'd rebelled because William's war hadn't been fair, because ransoming Anglo-Saxon lands and then making the nobles pay to get those lands back hadn't been fair—and above all else, William's eye-watering taxes were so unfair that the priest speaking to them actually started crying as he described them.

And honestly, Adelais had to agree about all the fairness, or lack thereof. She would have rebelled, too, in their shoes.

"I think," she told the king, "that it is cheaper to buy their loyalty now than to pay with more men and gold later when they decide to rebel again. Unhappy people will always want to rebel if they get the chance. But unhappy people having their purses emptied by your soldiers every time you need to raise funds? They will *make* the time to cause you trouble."

He'd looked at her. "I expected you to tell me to cut off the hands of their leaders and throw all the men in prison."

She'd looked at the emissaries then—priests and burghers

and barely blooded nobles. "There is no honor in that. We should play fair with them, as they have asked, and then maybe they will play fair with us." She'd paused. "And if they don't, you can cut off their hands then."

William had laughed, a short, cold noise that visibly chilled the people from Exeter, but they left the tent happy. In exchange for their allegiance, he'd not only lowered the taxes to what they'd been before Harold Godwinson's time, but had also forbidden his soldiers from doing any raiding or looting in the city. He'd even posted his best men as guards at the gates to catch any Normans sneaking in to do mischief.

And as Adelais lay in her tent that night, she thought about how she'd arrogantly told Tate she herself always fought fair. She'd proclaimed it with swagger, like it was the truest thing in the world—and it *had* felt like the truest thing in the world when she said it, because she was thinking of a particular kind of fighting. A sword and an axe, arrows and knives. When it came to war and terror, she'd made sure whoever she set her sights on was ready and able to fight her back. She took pride in it.

But conquering wasn't just blood and fire, not if it was going to last. It was forcing fealty from the conquered; it was leveraging their assets or familial loyalties against them. It was replacing Anglo-Saxon nobles with Norman ones and changing the taxes and courts and laws that bound those nobles and all the people underneath them. If all of that was *conquering*, then it was rather stupid to say that Adelais always fought fair when half the battles were fought not with swords, but with writs and decrees and muttered commands from an impatient king.

And when it had come to Far Hope, Adelais had not fought fair at all. She'd hidden the truth—she'd lied. And something was very wrong with her if the woman she adored trusted Adelais to hunt her in the dark and take her on the road, but not to protect the one thing she cared about above all else.

She'd fucked this all up. She'd fucked it up and she had no idea how to fix it that wouldn't get her own hands chopped off.

Or worse—Tate's.

Adelais frowned at the sloping cloth roof of her tent, illuminated only by a small fire for the watchmen outside. Thinking of Tate being hurt made her miserable. Knowing that *she'd* hurt Tate was unbearable. It made her chest ache, like something large and sharp had gotten lodged in her throat. Only one other person had ever made her feel like this, and that was her son. From the moment he'd blinked up at her with dark, nearly unseeing eyes—his squished little face still glistening with blood and his mouth opening for a battle cry that would have made even seasoned Danes turn and run for cover—she'd known she would destroy anything that so much as touched a single hair on his head.

And though what she felt for Tate was far from maternal, she could recognize it now, however shocking it was.

She loved Tate, abbess of Far Hope Abbey. She loved the stubborn, composed, secretly wicked woman, and she had to make this right for her.

And maybe Tate would never love her back, not after this. But that wasn't the point.

The point was that she was going to start playing fair. For Tate, for Far Hope. For everyone who'd ever found happiness under the starlike ceiling of its secret chambers.

And that would have to be enough.

Twelve

TATE

WYNFLAED and the others arrived back a week later, although much of the abbey's treasure remained at Thornchurch until Tate could decide what to do with it. It was simply too tempting a prospect here at the abbey, and the last thing she needed was their purse lightened by a money-hungry William or an acquisitive wolf.

Tate welcomed Wynflaed gratefully and even gave her a hug.

Wynflaed pulled back after they'd embraced, eyes wide. "Tate," she said. "You just *hugged* me."

"It's been a long two weeks," said Tate, trying to keep her voice neutral and failing.

And then—horribly—her face crumpled. She felt it happen. She hated it. And yet she couldn't stop it.

She put her hands to her face and wept harder than she ever had in her life, including after she'd killed Cafnoth, while Wynflaed folded her into her arms.

"It's all right," Wynflaed crooned. "I'm here. I'm here."

Why hadn't Tate ever let anyone comfort her before? It felt nice. Warm. The loneliness, the heartbreak, and the weight of the abbey's future receded a little bit. But as she pressed her face in Wynflaed's shoulder and sobbed, she couldn't help but wish it was someone else's shoulder instead. Someone who smelled like metal and grass, whose soft, red hair would tickle her face. Someone who would kiss her—and then bite her. Or the other way around.

She missed Adelais, no matter how foolish it was. And even more foolish was the skip of her heart when she remembered that she would *have* to see Adelais again if Adelais was their patron and landholder. She'd have to see those gold eyes, those freckles the color of dried blood. That beautiful, lying mouth.

Somehow, unwillingly, Tate found the whole story sliding out. From her first night with the Wolf, to her meeting with King William in the Wolf's tent. How she started her arrangement with Adelais to keep the abbey safe, and somehow lost her heart instead.

"I only knew her three days," Tate sniffled, chin still dimpling with tears. "How can it matter so much?"

"We've seen people fall in love in less, haven't we?" Wynflaed soothed, stroking her hair. "After only a day. After only a few hours. Why not you?"

"Because I'm more sensible than that!" Tate protested through wet gulps of air. "Because I know better than to fall in love with a lying Norman who wants to take control of Far Hope!"

"Oh, Tate," sighed Wynflaed. "We already knew Far Hope was coming to an end eventually. Maybe it's time to admit that to ourselves and figure out what's next."

Tate pulled away, wiping her face. "But it's not supposed to happen like this," she said, voice trembling. "I always thought that...well, that the sisters would go one by one and

I'd die here alone. Or something. The last one to keep the braziers burning."

Wynflaed rolled her eyes. "Tate, that's very songlike and all, but you didn't think that would actually happen, right? They shut down abbeys left and right these days—because some bishop decides to use the land for some other abbey's income or because someone founds a new abbey and everyone leaves to join it. They'll close Far Hope long before you die alone, entombed by ancient secrets or however you want this song of yours to end."

Tate sniffled again. Now that Wynflaed was saying this, she supposed the image in her head had been rather...dramatic. And maybe she had been clinging to the songlike idea of it because it was all she had left. If she couldn't hold this abbey together and keep it going, if she was responsible for yet another death, of a sort, then at least it should be a noble one. A stoic one. At least she wouldn't have made anyone else suffer with her.

Except now she was crying and snotty and not stoic at all.

So what did she have left?

Wynflaed hugged her again. "I bet the pagans here felt the same way when the Christians came, and I bet the Christians who still practiced the old ways felt the same when King Alfred decided to build an abbey here. And yet through all those changes, Far Hope has kept its heart. We must believe Far Hope can do it again."

Tate nodded against her friend's arm and started crying even harder, because hope stung so, so much worse than defeat.

* * *

Six weeks later, Tate was walking home from Thornchurch, a crown of tightly furled roses in her hand. She visited her childhood home every year for the first of May, and so she'd just come from Beltane, her stomach full of good food and her mood enlivened somewhat by all the dancing and merrymaking. Not that she'd made merry much herself, but it was still nice to be around. Ongoing strife and famine had dried up the slow trickle of Far Hope's pilgrims entirely; the cave with its quartz ceiling and burning braziers hadn't been used since Candlemas, in February. Tate's days were spent praying—matins, lauds, vespers, compline—and working. Cleaning the abbey, gardening, sewing, gathering eggs and milk.

Waiting for the inevitable: when Adelais would return and begin closing William's fist over the abbey at last.

But when she thought about it—and she did have lots of time to think these days, since her hours were spent kneeling in vegetable beds or gathering fresh rushes for the floor or singing songs she'd sung hundreds and hundreds of times before—it wasn't entirely fair to blame Adelais for the inevitable end of the abbey, not when even Mother Ardith had seen it coming. They'd opened the cave in February, yes, but before that, it had gone unused since September. When Tate had finally been shown Far Hope's secrets seven years ago, pilgrims had been taken to the cave two or three times a month. And now it was barely twice a year.

Perhaps King Alfred had only forestalled what had been slowly dying for centuries, had bellowed air into Far Hope's dying lungs so it could live on for a couple centuries more.

She could not lay that at Adelais's feet. In truth, she'd rather have Adelais as the abbey's landholder than anyone else, and maybe that was God's one blessing to Tate and the sisters now. If it should be anyone, it should be Adelais.

She still wished Adelais had told her the truth. She still wished Adelais had promised to help her make it all better.

She still...well. It didn't matter that she still loved Adelais, did it? Not when all of this stretched between them. Not when she was a nun and Adelais was William's wolf. Not when Adelais wasn't here in the valley at all.

Though the air had grown milder, warmer, the days weren't to their summer length yet, and the shadows began stretching out while Tate was still a handful of miles from Far Hope. Another hour and it was gloaming, with the pink-orange light getting darker and bluer the farther she walked.

Finally, it was just her in the dark with her crown of roses. She tried not to think of that night on this very same road, of how hard she came. Of how the Wolf's weight on her felt like an embrace, like the only thing that could set her free. She tried not to think of the Wolf's honest, vulnerable confessions, the many wolves inside the one copper-haired warrior.

She failed. And with a deep sigh, she let her mind—and her heart—return to memories of Adelais, since memories were all she had now. Adelais hadn't come to the abbey once since William gave her its lands, and even if she did return, Tate didn't know what she'd do. She was still angry at Adelais...even as she also wanted Adelais to build a house within sight of the abbey and spend every waking minute with Tate. Ideally in Tate's bed. Or in between the braziers.

She wanted to see all the different ways Adelais was and could be. She wanted forever, even if she were angry forever.

Which maybe she wouldn't be. Holding the fading flower crown, alone on the road with only the owls for company, it all seemed so pointless now. The abbey was nearing the end of its days with or without a new landlord. At least she could be grateful that her new landlord was so very pretty to look at.

Footsteps came behind Tate, and she whirled, lifting the heavy stick she'd been using to walk with.

"Stop!" she ordered the fast-moving shape behind her, and to her surprise, the shape stopped.

Tate stared.

"I told you I'd stop whenever you asked me to," came a

low, burned-edges voice. A cloud shifted above, revealing a tall person with scarlet hair and eerie gold eyes.

Tate's heart leapt—and then crashed.

"What are you doing here?" she asked.

"I saw you on the road, and I thought I'd make sure you got home safe," Adelais said.

"I'll be home safe," Tate said, already forcing herself to turn away. She couldn't be near Adelais, couldn't handle the sight of her, not when all she wanted was to fall at her feet and press her face into Adelais's thighs. "You can go."

"I'm sorry," Adelais said quickly. Clumsily. Like it was the first time she'd ever uttered the phrase. When Tate turned back to look at her, she said it again.

Slower now, with her eyes on Tate's.

"I'm sorry I didn't tell you that William was going to gift me with Far Hope. I'm sorry that I wasn't worthy of the things you showed me."

Tate searched Adelais's moon-washed face, stared right into those bright eyes as the apology hung in the sweet spring air. An apology that Tate never thought she'd hear, an apology she'd thought it impossible for this roguish, swaggering soldier to give.

But she *had* given it—unprompted, unsought. With nothing offered in return.

"And I want to help fix it," Adelais rushed in, mistaking Tate's attention for doubt. "I am sorry, and I want to make it right. I want to play fair with you for real now."

Tate stepped a little closer, still studying her. "You really do mean it?"

A line appeared between Adelais's brows. "My apology?"

"Yes."

"Of course I mean it. Knowing that I hurt you felt awful. I should have been honest with you from the beginning."

Tate closed her eyes, something loosening in her chest.

Like when Wynflaed held her as she wept, except even stronger this time. Like her whole body could turn itself into light, into a thousand points of it, like the stars at night.

Maybe this had been what she'd needed all along, since the start of the war, since she killed Cafnoth as a scared young woman. Someone to say *I'm sorry this hurts; I'm sorry you're hurting*.

Someone to say *I'm sorry and I won't let you hurt alone*.

"Thank you," Tate murmured. And then she opened her eyes. "I forgive you, Adelais."

In the moonlight, she could see the new shine of tears in Adelais's gold eyes, and Tate was filled with so much tenderness, she didn't know if she could speak.

"Thank you," Adelais said huskily. "And I meant what I said. About playing fair now. I want to prove it to you, no matter how long it takes."

"That's one of the things I love about you," she managed, and Adelais's face opened with delight.

"You love things about me?" the Wolf asked, sounding giddy.

"I love you," Tate said softly, simply, knowing it to be as true as the earth beneath her feet, as true as God himself.

Adelais shifted in place, her hands flexing, and Tate said, "You don't have to stop anymore. You can come closer."

Adelais moved fast enough to drive the wind from Tate's lungs, wrapping her strong arms around Tate and crushing her close.

"I love you too," whispered the Wolf. "I love you and I can't think of anyone or anything else. Be mine. Be mine for as long as you want."

Tate laughed, pressed her forehead to Adelais's before pulling away to look up at her. "I'm an abbess first, remember? I'm Far Hope's."

"What if I'm Far Hope instead?" Adelais asked, and Tate sighed.

"That's a sweet idea, but—"

"I have an idea," Adelais said suddenly. "For the abbey."

"Please don't feel like you have to—"

"What if we made a new Far Hope," Adelais said. "A new version of it like King Alfred did. Something that looks completely different but has the same heart underneath."

Tate stilled, unsure of what Adelais was saying.

Adelais bit her full lower lip. It almost looked bashful on the seasoned warrior. "Like me," she added. "Different Adelais, same heart."

A ball lodged in Tate's throat. But a good one, made of something bright and *happy*. Made of loving her wolf.

"If I'm the lord of Far Hope—in practice, if not in name—then we could keep people coming to the cave." Adelais went on, excited now, bouncing on the balls of her feet. "We could keep people coming on Christmas and Michaelmas and Martinmas and any other feast day you wanted. They'll simply be my guests, and no one need be any wiser. It'll be like how the pilgrimages work now: a truth that disguises the bigger truth. And instead of the abbey closing and not having anyone left to share its secrets—and instead of doing anything to provoke William's wrath—we'll turn ourselves into something so common no one pays any attention to them: naughty, misbehaving nobles."

Tate took Adelais's hand and squeezed it. "There will be no one to carry it on after we die," she tried to explain.

"Not true," Adelais said. "My son will inherit these lands. Perhaps after we die, we'll arrange to have him told the true nature of the place."

"That his inheritance is a hidden chamber for holy sex?"

Adelais shrugged. "He'll have to learn which accounts are overdue and which fields are actually bogs in any event;

learning about King Alfred's favorite sex shrine will be much more interesting."

Adelais had Tate there.

"It's supposed to be a sacred place," Tate finally said. "Set apart from ordinary life. How can a house—even a fine house belonging to a noble—be sacred? Set apart enough that people can be and change in ways they can't in their daily lives?"

"Didn't you tell me that you didn't make those distinctions? Anything we want to be holy can be? We can keep the church open as a local church; we can welcome visitors to the healing spring. You are the pious lifeblood of the abbey, Tate, you and your strength and your belief in this place. You will bring that piety to a new Far Hope too."

Tate thought.

And thought.

It could work.

But should it? Should a place that had always been different, divine, liminal become something as common and transient as a *house*?

It wouldn't be just any house. It would belong to Adelais of the Maine.

Adelais, who was different and divine all on her own. Adelais, who was ready to play fair, Adelais, who knew more than anyone else how important having a place set apart from the world's expectations could be.

The breeze blew between them, around them, and Adelais bit Tate's jaw once, hard. The pain lanced through her chest down to her cunt, and she shivered.

"I suppose we could try..." Tate said slowly, and that mischievous grin returned. "And," Tate added as the Wolf pulled her close and started rucking up her gown, searching for her nakedness, "we'll have to have rules. Like we do now at the abbey: rules for working hours, silent hours, for how we get along together. Only for...whatever this will be."

"Hmm, how about," Adelais murmured, "no rules at all?" Her fingers searched out Tate's bare cunt and stroked.

"There have to be rules," Tate managed to squeak out.

"Fine," Adelais said, sounding distracted. She slid two fingers inside Tate, and Tate shuddered. She'd give the Wolf anything she wanted right now. Anything at all. "How about: no law but pleasure."

"I like that," Tate said as Adelais pressed the heel of her palm to Tate's clitoris, sending plenty of pleasure through Tate's body.

"And no limit but acquiescence." Adelais began fucking Tate hard, which Tate acquiesced to with nods and groans and *yeses*. It was right to do this here in the dark, on the road where they'd played their game. It was right to match promises with shivers and honesty and short, sharp gasps.

It was right to burn away the last six weeks with these dazzling, searing moments together.

"And," Tate said breathlessly, "secrecy. We can't forget that."

"Of course not, abbess. Spread your legs farther apart."

Tate did as she was asked and was rewarded for it, with Adelais going deeper and faster, making sure to give her aching bundle of nerves as much attention as it needed.

"It'll be a little kingdom of our own," the Wolf promised the abbess as she began to reach a clawing orgasm. "Our own little world."

"Yes," panted Tate, racked with the onslaught of her peak. "Yes."

A smile in the dark before Tate was pushed to her knees and Adelais shoved her hose down to reveal where she wanted Tate's mouth.

"And it shall be *beautiful*."

The end.

*** * ***

Want more dangerous widowers, gothic houses, and carnal secrets from Sierra Simone?

Check out the completely free book The Awakening of Ivy Leavold!

WANT MORE FROM SIERRA SIMONE?

Want more from Sierra Simone?

Want more dangerously possessive lovers, gothic settings, and carnal secrets from Sierra Simone?

Check out The Chasing of Eleanor Vane!

Ajax Dartham, the Duke of Jarrell, has a problem. And that problem is his future niece-in-law.

When the clever and capable Lady Eleanor Vane—understandably—runs off into the night rather than marry his horrible nephew, the Duke has a choice.

Should he catch Eleanor and return her to her fate—**or make Eleanor his own instead?**

Grab this quick and dirty age gap romance today!

Also by Sierra Simone

Co-Written with Julie Murphy:

A Merry Little Meet Cute

Snow Place Like LA: A Christmas in July Novella

A Holly Jolly Ever After

The Lyonesse Trilogy:

Salt in the Wound (a free Lyonesse prequel!)

Salt Kiss

Honey Cut

Lyonesse #3

Standalones:

Red & White: an FFM winter story — FREE!

Supplicant: an age gap novella

Sanguine: an MM vampire story

Sherwood: an FFM novella

My Present This Year: a forbidden Christmas story - FREE!

The Priest Series:

Priest

Midnight Mass: A Priest Novella

Sinner

Saint

Thornchapel:

A Lesson in Thorns

Feast of Sparks

Harvest of Sighs

Door of Bruises

Misadventures:

Misadventures with a Professor

Misadventures of a Curvy Girl

Misadventures in Blue

The New Camelot Trilogy:

American Queen

American Prince

American King

The Moon (Merlin's Novella)

American Squire (A Thornchapel and New Camelot Crossover)

High Spice Historicals:

The Markham Hall Series

The Awakening of Ivy Leavold

The Education of Ivy Leavold

The Punishment of Ivy Leavold

The London Lovers

The Seduction of Molly O'Flaherty

The Wedding of Molly O'Flaherty

Far Hope Stories

The Chasing of Eleanor Vane

The Last Crimes of Peregrine Hind

The Conquering of Tate the Pious

Co-Written with Laurelin Paige

Porn Star

Hot Cop

About the Author

Sierra Simone is a USA Today bestselling former librarian who spent too much time reading romance novels at the information desk. She lives with her husband and family in Kansas City.

Sign up for her newsletter to be notified of releases, books going on sale, events, and other news!

www.thesierrasimone.com
thesierrasimone@gmail.com

www.ingramcontent.com/pod-product-compliance
Lightning Source LLC
Chambersburg PA
CBHW010558170726
48285CB00011B/2965